A kiss that could destroy a lifetime of well-laid plans...

He slid his fingers through her hair, tilting her face up to his. And then he kissed her, taking his time—a slow, languorous touch of mouth against mouth, tongue against tongue, building in increments of heat and desire until he found she was trembling, and he was, too.

He didn't ask. He simply pulled her up tight against his body and took her to bed. And she let him....

Dear Reader,

This year, 1999, is a special one for Harlequin. It marks the 50th anniversary of the company that each and every month brings you the best in romance fiction.

And following that golden tradition, we're thrilled to publish Anne Stuart's latest novel. This is a special book to Anne, because she wrote it as a tribute to Harlequin's 50th anniversary.

The incomparable Anne Stuart has become synonymous with sizzling romance. She published her first book in 1974, and in the over fifty novels and countless short stories since then, she has demonstrated an uncanny ability to touch readers with witty repartee, heartfelt emotional drama and her trademark sexual tension. Anne has won every major writing award, including three prestigious RITA Awards from the Romance Writers of America and, in 1996, a Lifetime Achievement Award. She lives in Vermont, with her husband, daughter and son.

Happy reading!

Debra Matteucci
Senior Editor & Editorial Coordinator
Harlequin Books
300 E. 42nd St.
New York, NY 10017

Anne Stuart

THE RIGHT MAN

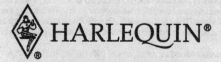

HARLEQUIN®

TORONTO • NEW YORK • LONDON
AMSTERDAM • PARIS • SYDNEY • HAMBURG
STOCKHOLM • ATHENS • TOKYO • MILAN • MADRID
PRAGUE • WARSAW • BUDAPEST • AUCKLAND

ISBN 0-373-16765-2

THE RIGHT MAN

Part One—Susan

Chapter One

Susan Abbott of the Connecticut Abbotts had always been the perfect daughter. A good, clever, ambitious, dutiful girl, and it had all come down to five days before her wedding to possibly the most eligible bachelor in Connecticut, and she was in the midst of a completely uncharacteristic temper tantrum. "I hate this dress!" She tugged at the frilly white flounce adorning her hips as she stared in the mirror and bit her lip. She wasn't used to letting irrational emotions make her snappish, and she never snapped at her mother.

"Don't pull at it," Mary Abbott protested. "If you rip it Edward's mother will never forgive you."

"If I rip it maybe I won't have to wear it," Susan said mutinously. "One can only hope." She turned sideways, looking at her reflection in the godawful dress. She wasn't one to worry obsessively about her clothes, but this piece of frou-frou was exactly what she didn't want to get married in. Everything about her wedding was going to be perfect, simple and elegant, except for this monstrosity foisted upon her by Edward's mother, Vivian. She suspected her reluctant mother-in-law took a perverse pleasure in making her future daughter-in-law look foolish.

It had hoop skirts, for heaven's sake! It had layers and layers of polyester lace, so that she looked like an upside-down ice-cream cone. It had short puffy sleeves that were too tight, a neckline that flattened what cleavage she had, and it itched.

But Vivian Jeffries had worn it forty years ago when she married her poor, henpecked husband, and it was her fondest wish that her future daughter-in-law wear it when she married Vivian's beloved only child, Edward. How could she refuse? Particularly since Vivian was doing a stalwart job of covering up her sincere belief that Edward was far too good for even an Abbott of Connecticut.

There didn't seem to be any way around the problem of the dress—neither Susan nor Mary had been able to come up with a reasonable excuse. Mary Abbott had eloped: her wedding dress was a Dior suit from the late fifties that would scarcely fit her tall daughter.

And while Vivian now carried an impressive bulk on her matronly frame, she'd been reed slim when she'd married, and Susan would eat nails before she admitted that it was too tight.

She took a step backward, peering at herself in the mirror. "Maybe if we got rid of the hoop skirts," she murmured, not hopeful.

"They need to hold up the train," Mary said.

"There's a train, too? Merciful heavens," Susan said faintly. "I don't suppose we could elope?"

"Vivian would never forgive you."

"I don't think Vivian's going to forgive me for stealing her devoted son from her," Susan muttered.

"Besides, the wedding is less than a week away. You've spent an enormous amount of money already—I can't imagine you'd want to throw it all away at this late date."

"The rest of you can stay and party. Edward and I can run away, and I won't have to wear this horrible dress," she suggested, knowing it was a lost cause. Despite her protests, Mary deserved to have her daughter suitably wed in a manner that would return them to the forefront of Matchfield society.

Mary shook her head. "I'll support whatever decision you make. But this isn't like you, to get so upset over a silly dress."

"I've never been married before." Susan sighed.

"It's not that bad, darling. Besides, brides are always beautiful." For a moment Mary looked misty-eyed.

"If only you'd had a formal wedding I'd have the perfect excuse not to wear this." Susan wasn't about to wonder what else it might give her an excuse not to do—that was far too dangerous. If Mary Abbott had married the right man in the first place, instead of a ne'er-do-well drunk like Alex Donovan, then maybe it wouldn't matter if Susan married someone a little less suitable than Edward Jeffries, a little less perfect.

Not that there was anyone else she wanted to marry. All her life she'd been searching for stability, permanence. To become a real Abbott once more. Dear, devoted Edward was the key to that. She'd made her choice, set her course years ago. It was too late to change her mind, just when she was about to get everything she ever wanted.

"You're five inches taller than I am, Susan," Mary said, oblivious to her convoluted train of thought. "Even if I had something for you to wear it would never fit. And after your aunt's death I'm afraid the family wouldn't have been able to handle another formal wedding, even if they'd approved of my choice."

Susan presented her back to her mother. "Maybe I'll be lucky and die on my wedding day like Aunt Tallulah. Then I won't have to wear this thing."

"Susan!" Mary admonished her, shocked. "She was my sister, you know."

Susan bit her lip, ashamed. She spun around. "I'm sorry, Mother. I'm being a spoiled brat, and you don't deserve it. I know you still miss her after all these years...."

"She died fifty years ago, sweetie. I was only nine. Yes, I still miss her, but I've gotten over it," Mary said calmly, pulling at the zipper. "Damn," she muttered. "I think it's stuck."

The polyester lace was giving Susan a rash, the

zipper was digging into her spine, she'd been on a diet for two weeks and she was not in a good mood. To top it off, the doorbell rang.

"Susan!" Mary admonished her daughter's hearty curse. "Just stay there and I'll see who it is. Probably more wedding gifts."

"More Steuben bud vases and espresso machines," Susan moaned, tugging at the dress. "Just what I need."

She flounced back to the mirror as her mother disappeared, staring at her reflection. She was tall, five feet nine and a half, and her body was lean rather than curvy. Her thick, honey-colored hair was cut short, waving around her strong, angular face, and her green eyes were wary. She wasn't a soft, pretty woman, she was slender and strong with her own sense of style. She was definitely not made for ruffles and lace.

She yanked again, getting nowhere, when she heard her mother's voice, soft and faintly breathless, talking to someone.

"I'm sure Susan won't mind if you come along in. We're having a little trouble with the dress...."

She saw him first in the mirror, towering over her diminutive mother. For a brief, startled moment she met his gaze, and then she turned, yanking the dress back up around her shoulders.

He looked like a cross between Indiana Jones and an aging hippie. He was somewhere in his mid-thirties, deeply tanned, his shaggy hair sun streaked, his blue eyes light in his dark face. He was wearing travel-stained khakis that could probably raise a cloud of dust, he hadn't shaved in several days, and he wore an amulet of some sort around his neck. Susan just looked at him in astonishment.

"Susan, this is a friend of your godmother's, Jake… I'm afraid I've forgotten your last name," Mary said, Mary whose command of social niceties was inbred, Mary who never forgot a name. She was looking oddly pleased to see him.

"Jake Wyczynski," he said in a deep, drawling voice. "I don't blame you for having trouble with it."

"And this is the bride herself. Jake's brought presents from your godmother, Louisa."

Susan held out one hand, holding the dress up with the other. "I wish you'd brought my godmother," she said ruefully. "I'm thirty years old and I've never even met her."

He had a strong, hard hand and a good grip. "Louisa's a character," he said. "Never stays in one place for long, I'm afraid. She wanted to come for your wedding, but she's still in the middle of her funeral journey, so she sent me in her place."

"Funeral journey?" Susan echoed, astonished.

"Her husband died last year, and she's scattering a little of his ashes at each of their special places. Considering that they spent their lives traveling the globe, it's taking her some time." He tilted his head sideways. "Are you having trouble with that dress?"

"The zipper's stuck."

"Let me try it."

She hesitated. She was only wearing the skimpiest of bra and panties beneath the hated dress, and for some reason she didn't want his hands on her bare skin. Big, strong hands.

"Yes, let him," Mary said. "I've given up."

With a sigh she presented her back to him, holding her breath. She could see him in the mirror, his shaggy head bent, she could feel his warm breath on her back, his fingers as he touched the dress.

"Sure is stuck," he murmured. "The zipper's a little rusty."

"It's an old dress," Susan muttered.

"I figured it must be. You wouldn't have chosen it if it didn't have some sentimental meaning." His fingers brushed against her skin, and she jumped.

"It doesn't have any sentimental meaning for me," she said. "It's my fiancé's mother's dress. I hate it."

"Do you?" He smelled like sun and wind, she thought abstractedly. Edward always smelled like designer cologne.

"I'd give anything not to have to wear it..." Her voice trailed off at the sound of polyester ripping.

He stepped back, an enigmatic expression on his face. "Sorry," he said. "I think I ruined it."

The dress had fallen down around her, and she only managed to preserve her modesty by clutching it to her. She whirled around to survey the damage.

It was ruined, all right. Ripped from bodice almost all the way to the hem, and not a nice, neat tear along the seam. He'd managed to destroy it with one yank.

"Oh, my heavens," Mary murmured, aghast.

Susan turned back, stunned, the ruined dress clutched around her. And then she laughed out loud, unable to help herself. "It's ruined. You've just given me the best wedding gift of all. I hope you're planning on staying for the ceremony?"

"I wouldn't miss it for the world. I promised your godmother I'd give her a full report," he said in a lazy drawl.

"Let me make arrangements for a place for you to stay..." Mary began, but he shook his head.

"Don't worry about me, ma'am," he said. "I've already taken care of that. I promised Louisa I'd drop off the first present as soon as I got here, but then I'll make myself scarce."

"The first present?"

"It's a tradition in one of the nomadic tribes Louisa and her husband used to travel with. The bride receives gifts from a wise woman every day for a week before the wedding. I left the first one in the hallway."

"But I haven't offered you any refreshment," Mary protested. "What about dinner tonight...?"

"I'll just see to myself, ma'am, but thank you, anyway. I'll come by tomorrow with the next present if you don't have any objections. Louisa's counting on me."

"And you seem very reliable, Mr. Wyczynski," Mary said warmly.

"Call me Jake. It's a hell of a lot easier on the tongue. Nice meeting you, Susan."

He was the epitome of old-fashioned courtesy, distant and charming. "Thanks for the dress," she said.

"Anytime."

The moment she heard the front door close she let the dress fall on the floor, stepping out of it and kicking it away from her. "There's no chance it can be fixed in time, is there?" she asked her mother in a hopeful voice when Mary returned.

"I doubt it. He did a thorough job of mangling it."

"Bless his heart," Susan said cheerfully. "I wonder if he's got a suit he can wear for the wedding? That big-white-hunter gear might look a little strange for an afternoon garden wedding."

"He's not going to fit in, anyway, Susan," Mary said with a trace of sharpness in her voice. "I don't know why you'd worry about such things."

"I'm not worried. He's very colorful."

"He's very handsome," her mother said.

"Is he? I didn't notice."

"You never could lie to me, Susan."

Susan smiled ruefully. "No, I couldn't. Yes, he's gorgeous, but as you know, he's hardly my type. I tend to go for more civilized men, like Edward. And besides, he didn't show the faintest bit of interest in me, at least, not as a woman."

"You're engaged to be married, Susan. He'd hardly be flirting with you."

"He did rip my dress off. Bless him," she added. "Don't look so worried, mother. I'm not about to change my mind about Edward at this late date. He and I were meant for each other, and we've known that since we were in college. This is an entirely logical next step in our relationship."

"And you'll give me entirely logical grandchildren before long?"

"Don't hold your breath. Edward thinks we should be more settled in our careers."

Mary's smile seemed a little tight. "And Edward's always right."

"Yes, he is. One of his annoying habits." Susan pulled on a faded pair of jeans and an old cotton sweater. "Don't worry, I know you adore him. There'll be plenty of grandchildren soon enough. I've only just begun to hear my biological clock ticking."

"You have?" Mary looked oddly hopeful. "I didn't know you'd even thought about children."

"I've thought about them. I'll be ready when Edward is."

"I'm relieved to hear that," Mary said in an even voice. "In the meantime, what are we going to do about this dress?" She scooped it off the floor and shook it. "I don't mind telling you I'd rather not be the one to spring the word on Vivian. She's even more formidable than her son."

"She is, isn't she? Edward's a pussycat if you

know how to handle him, and he absolutely idolizes you, Mother. People only think he's a barracuda because he's a Wall Street lawyer. He's perfect husband material, and we're going to be deliriously happy.''

''Of course you are,'' Mary said, her back turned.

''Don't worry, I'll find some way to tell Vivian about her dress. Not right away, though—she's capable of finding someone who can fix the wretched thing on short notice. In the meantime we've got to figure out what I'll wear. I imagine I can find something off the rack if I have to.''

''Let's have a cup of tea and see what Louisa has sent you. She always had the most extraordinary taste,'' Mary said. ''We can worry about a dress later.''

''We have five days, Mother.''

''An hour won't make any difference one way or the other. And I'm making you herbal tea. You're getting too cranky,'' Mary said smartly.

''No honey,'' Susan said.

''You're too thin already,'' Mary overruled her. ''You'll have honey and cake. I'm your mother and I still have some rights.''

''Yes, Mother,'' Susan said meekly.

The box was in the hallway where he'd left it. It was flat and rectangular, covered with crumpled brown paper, tied with string, looking rather as if it had been through the wars and back. Susan hefted it, surprised at how light it was.

"What do you suppose it could be?" She carried it into the living room of her mother's neat little house and sat on the floor with it. One of the first things Susan planned on doing after her marriage was to move her mother to better, more elegant surroundings, preferably the sprawling faux Tudor mansion that Edward had bought for them. She didn't expect to run into any opposition from her new husband— Edward was in awe of his delicate, future mother-in-law, and he was as practical about their marriage as Susan was. The house was huge—there was no reason why they couldn't share it.

"Something interesting, I have no doubt," Mary said, handing her a pair of scissors.

It took Susan less than a minute to rip off the layers of wrapping to expose the box beneath it. It was a dressmaker's box, very old, with a card taped on top of it. Even though she'd never met her legendary godmother, Susan recognized her handwriting.

She opened the note. "A token of your family's past, my dear. Despite what they tell you, good things happen to those who wear this."

"Cryptic as ever," Mary said, reading it over her shoulder. "Let's see what she's sent you. Probably some East Indian shroud of some sort."

Susan opened the box, pushing away the layers of tissue paper to expose yards and yards of creamy white satin.

"Oh, my heavens," Mary cried, and sank into a nearby chair.

Susan cast a curious glance at her mother as she pulled the dress out. It was a wedding dress made of rich, glossy satin, cut like a gown for a medieval princess, with laced-up sleeves and bodice and a long sweep of skirt. It had to be the most beautiful, unsuitable dress she'd ever seen, and she loved it.

She turned to her mother. "What's wrong?" she demanded.

"It's Tallulah's wedding dress," Mary said in a faint voice. "I always wondered what happened to it."

Susan rose, holding the dress up against her long body, unable to resist the impulse. It flowed against her, draping in graceful folds. "She must have been tall."

"She was. Tallulah towered over almost everyone. She looked so beautiful in that dress." Mary's voice caught for a moment. "Imagine Louisa having it all this time."

Susan stared at her reflection for a long, meditative moment. "It's obviously a sign," she said finally. "I'm meant to wear this dress."

"Don't be ridiculous, Susan!" her mother protested, shocked. "You can't possibly! It's bad luck. There's too much history...."

"Why? She didn't die in the dress, did she? You told me she was killed in a train wreck on her honeymoon."

"Her honeymoon hadn't even started," Mary said quietly. "They were on their way to New York to begin their trip to England. They were going to spend several months just touring Europe when it happened."

"You mean she didn't even have a wedding night?"

"No," Mary said shortly.

"She died a virgin? How completely depressing!"

Her mother cast her a stern glance. "Your generation didn't invent sex, you know."

"You mean Aunt Tallulah did the nasty with Neddie Marsden? Hard to believe, looking at him now. I can't believe anyone would want to sleep with him."

"Your aunt Tallulah was an original, Susan. She always followed her own heart, and if she loved someone, she loved them wholeheartedly, without reservation," Mary said. "She was never one to be bound by the restrictions of society."

"Even though she was an Abbott of Connecticut?" Susan asked, running a reverent hand along the rich, creamy satin.

"Most particularly because she was an Abbott of Connecticut."

"I still can't see a free spirit like her married to a stuffed shirt like Ned Marsden. Or maybe it was her premature death that turned him into such a turnip."

"I'm afraid Neddie Marsden was always a turnip," Mary admitted. "His second wife is much better suited to him. He'd probably prefer to forget all about Tallulah.''

"His lost love," Susan murmured. "It's so romantic."

"I was a nine-year-old who lost her beloved older sister," Mary said. "I didn't find it the slightest bit romantic."

Susan bit her lip. "I'm sorry, Mother. I'm not usually so self-absorbed. I know you still miss her."

"Never mind, dear." Mary came and stood behind her, staring down at the dress with a faraway expression. "It's in the past, where it belongs. But how extraordinary that Louisa would have this dress."

"You told me she was Aunt Tallulah's best friend. That was why you made me her goddaughter, even though she's never even seen me."

"Exactly," Mary said. "So it shouldn't come as any surprise, really." She touched the thick satin. "Are you going to try it on, then?"

Susan hesitated, torn. "I shouldn't..."

"Of course you should. I think you're right—it's a sign. Why else would it show up today of all days? If it fits, you have my blessing. I'm sure it's what Louisa had in mind, the old devil."

"But what about the rest of the family?"

"No one will remember. Most everyone at that wedding is dead by now—after all it was fifty years ago. And I think Tallulah would want you to wear it." She reached down and picked it up, shaking out the folds. "I don't think it even needs pressing."

It slid over her body like warm water, accentuating her slender curves, flowing down her long legs. She looked at her reflection in the mirror, and she looked like a lost princess, wistful and serene. She looked like someone she'd known, long ago, a secret girl inside her woman's heart.

"It fits," she said. She picked up the soft drape of the skirt and let it fall through her fingers. "I'm wearing it."

And she imagined, somewhere in heaven, her wild aunt Tallulah laughed.

Chapter Two

The tumbledown garage was all that was left of the once-sprawling Abbott estate that had dominated the small, elite town of Matchfield. The mansion and most of its outbuildings had burned in the early sixties, and the rest of the acreage had been developed into tasteful little town houses and a few select enclaves for the very wealthy. The garage had been off at a distance, and it remained, on its island of land, deserted and abandoned in the overgrown forest that bordered the neatly landscaped lawns of Matchfield Commons.

Jake Wyczynski was used to roughing it, and this was the height of elegance compared to some places he'd stayed recently. The roof was mostly intact, as were the windows, there were only a few steps missing on the stairs, and the few pieces of furniture seemed basically sturdy. He threw open the windows, beat several pounds of dust off the thin mattress on the old iron bed and tossed his sleeping bag on top of it.

It would do for the next week. He'd promised Louisa, and he was a man who kept his promises. Besides, he owed Louisa more than his life, and he'd walk through fire for her. Attending a society wedding was almost as torturous, but for Louisa he could endure it.

He wondered what she would have thought of her goddaughter. Jake himself had been reluctantly impressed, which made his short exile in society both easier and more difficult. Susan Abbott was an amazon, tall and strong and graceful, even in that monstrosity of a dress. He would have been half tempted to rip the thing off her even if she'd professed to love it. Such a piece of tasteless fluff was an affront to his sense of beauty. Susan Abbott was a magnificent creature, and she needed magnificent clothes to show her distinctive looks to advantage. Magnificent clothes, or nothing at all.

She'd had smooth, creamy skin beneath that silly dress. He wondered what her fiancé was like, whether he would appreciate her, or whether he'd want her in polyester and ruffles. She looked a little like a sleeping beauty, chaste, elegant, unawakened. He couldn't imagine a red-blooded male who wouldn't want to waken her with something a lot more potent than a kiss.

It wasn't his business, of course. He was here for Louisa, here as a messenger boy. As soon as the wedding was over he could get back to wherever the spirit moved him. He wondered if cool, straitlaced

Susan Abbott had ever done a spontaneous thing in her entire life.

He was passing judgment, something he hated. People made their own choices, lived their own lives. It wasn't up to him to decide whether they were doing a good job of it or not.

Still, she looked as if there might be fire beneath her still exterior. She looked as if all her passion was carefully banked within that long, leggy body of hers. Maybe she was just waiting to be awakened.

Dangerous thoughts, and once again, none of his business. He didn't need to get emotionally involved with the Abbotts, and he certainly didn't need to get physically involved with a woman on the verge of her wedding.

He'd never been particularly interested in poaching on other people's relationships. But there was something about the calm clarity of Susan Abbott's eyes that called him.

He wasn't a man who noticed tiny physical details, but her vivid green eyes lingered in his mind. As did the small mole just below her shoulder blade, just above the lacy band of her skimpy bra.

He shook his head in disgust. Louisa would be sorely disappointed in him, for letting himself be distracted by her little goddaughter.

Except there was nothing little about Susan Abbott. And Louisa knew him too well to be surprised by anything. She had always had a healthy respect for natural human lust.

He threw himself down on the cot, and a cloud of dust rose beneath his sleeping bag, gold-flecked motes floating peacefully in the late-afternoon air. Sooner or later he'd go find himself some good old American fast food, maybe a beer as well. He might as well enjoy his exile for the short time it would last. Society had a few things to offer, including burgers and fries.

He could even indulge his fantasies, just a little bit, and no one would be any the wiser. He could stretch his body out and think of Susan Abbott. Whether she'd ever had anyone kiss that perfect little mole. What she'd look like when she came.

He lay back and grinned lazily. It was a harmless pastime, and she would never have the faintest idea he viewed her with anything more than dispassionate curiosity. He could carry the image of her back with him on his travels, standing there in the midst of her mother's living room, that mass of white lace falling off her creamy body. He had every intention of enjoying those memories thoroughly.

He sighed, tucking his arms behind his head as he surveyed the cobweb-festooned ceiling of the old building. Whichever of the Abbotts' faithful retainers had lived here, a generation ago, they obviously hadn't been interested in creature comforts. Neither was he.

The only creature comfort that lured him right now was a faint, betraying flash of lust for another man's bride.

SUSAN HAD PLANNED on telling Jake Wyczynski how grateful she was, both for his handy disposal of Vivian's wedding dress and the delivery of her late aunt Tallulah's gown, but he was nowhere to be seen the next day. It upset her plans. She found him slightly unsettling, and a friendly, formal meeting would put things back on the right footing.

But he didn't appear. A package showed up at her mother's doorstep, along with the latest offerings from FedEx and UPS, but Susan didn't waste her time with the traditional gifts. She went straight to the small, battered package, knowing instinctively it was from her godmother.

"What's she sent you now?" Mary looked up from her carefully ordered list of gifts. She'd been brought up to follow the niceties of society to a tee, and she wasn't about to fail at this critical juncture, the marriage of her only child.

"I haven't the faintest idea." Susan held up the intricate mesh of silver. It looked somewhat like a spiderweb, with beads scattered through it.

"Maybe Jake will know. We'll have to ask him next time we see him."

"I suppose," Susan said doubtfully. "You don't know where he's staying?"

Her mother shook her head no. "He told me Louisa arranged something for him."

"Maybe he's camping somewhere. He looks the type."

"I thought you used to like camping."

Susan squashed down the little trickle of guilt at her mother's hurt expression. "I liked camping with you, mother. Just the two of us, in the woods, not being Abbotts of Connecticut. I guess as I've gotten older I've learned to appreciate the glories of running water."

"Have you? Or is it Edward's civilized effect on you?"

Susan grinned. "I can't really see Edward roughing it, can you? I think he was born in a three-piece suit."

"I expect you've seen him without it at least on occasion," Mary said, a note of a question in her voice.

She could ignore it. She and her mother had an unspoken respect for each other's privacy, combined with a deep concern. Their lives had been so entwined, with no husband or father to interfere, that they'd almost developed a kind of mental shorthand. Mary had to have guessed, and she might as well be honest.

"I thought you knew," she said in a careless voice. "Edward thinks we should wait until we're married."

"Wait for what?"

"To sleep together. I thought you would have figured that out."

Mary Abbott's expression was blank, but Susan knew her mother far too well. "If that suits you, darling," she said. "I'm sure you're old enough to know your own mind."

Susan managed a careless little laugh. "It's not as if we both hadn't tried it in our misspent youth. And we're so attuned on everything else, we can't help but be compatible sexually."

"If you say so."

"You don't approve. I would have thought you'd be pleased. Edward is every mother's dream."

"I didn't say I didn't approve, Susan." Mary set the legal pad aside. "You know I love Edward dearly. I just want you to be very certain you know what you're doing."

"We're not going to end up like you and my father," Susan said, unable to keep the defensiveness out of her voice.

Mary's smile was rueful. "I'm sure you're not. Your father and I were completely at odds about everything. He liked the country, I liked the city, he was an intellectual, I was athletic. He liked to read, I liked to shop. It was a disaster from the word go, and no one was surprised when we divorced a few months after you were born."

"Did your parents approve?" Susan sat back on her heels, surveying her mother curiously. Mary Abbott could seldom be persuaded to talk about her short marriage, and Susan had been angry enough at her father for abandoning her not to push things. But now, as her life was about to change, she found she was curious.

"They approved of the divorce, not the marriage. Once I changed my name back to Abbott and refused to have anything to do with Alex then everything was fine." She sighed. "It's ancient history. I don't know why I even brought it up."

"Because we were talking about incompatibility. How Edward and I are made for each other," Susan prompted.

Mary's smile was faint. "Yes, darling. But no matter how far apart your father and I were in everything else, the sex was absolutely amazing."

"Too much information!" Susan said, covering her ears. "I don't want to envision my mother having sex, thank you very much."

"I didn't find you under a cabbage leaf, you know."

"You might as well have, since I had no father," she said frankly. Mary didn't even flinch. "Is that why you married him? Because the sex was good?" She wasn't sure she wanted to hear the answer.

"No, darling. I married him because I loved him, irrational as it was. And that's why the sex was good."

"Then I should have no problem," Susan said blithely.

"Because you love Edward." There was just the faint trace of a question in Mary's gentle voice.

"Of course. I'm marrying him, aren't I?"

"I thought it was more a practical than an emotional decision."

"Marriage should always be a practical decision," Susan said firmly. "It's too important an issue to let your emotions or your heart get in the way."

For a moment Mary looked stricken. "And you wouldn't want your heart to get in the way, would you, sweetheart?" she said softly.

She recognized the troubled tone in her mother's voice. "I love Edward," Susan repeated firmly. "Trust me."

"Always, darling. What are you going to wear to the Andersons' party tonight? They've invited just about everyone, I'm afraid, even though I told them that this week was hectic enough already."

"We'll survive. At least I'll have some time with Edward." She said it almost defiantly. She loved Edward, truly. If it wasn't the mad, passionate desire of a teenager, well, they were both too mature for that. She loved him in a calm, rational manner, secure in everything the future held for the two of them. She rose, heading toward her mother, and put a hand on her shoulder. "Trust me, mother. I know what I'm doing."

Mary smiled up at her, but there was no missing the real doubt in her warm blue eyes. "Of course, dear."

HER MOTHER WAS RIGHT: the Andersons' sprawling Tudor mansion was crammed with people. Susan had been trained by her mother in the fine art of social intercourse, and she survived a good three hours of chitchat, shrimp hors d'oeuvres, distant glimpses of Edward, and enough French champagne to fell a lesser woman. She'd learned how to sip, making one glass linger, she'd learned how to smile and look as if every word was utterly fascinating.

For some reason tonight it all felt particularly hollow.

She must have been overtired, she decided, making an automatically sympathetic response to Taylor Anderson's gastrointestinal woes. She'd been brought up for this sort of thing, she was good at it. Across the crowded room she could see Edward thriving, charming everyone who came within his orbit, and he was counting on her doing the same thing. For some reason she wasn't quite sure why she should.

It was a warm summer night in June. No one noticed when she slipped out onto the terrace, closing the French doors behind her. She took a deep breath of the damp night air, then looked down to discover her hands were shaking. Bridal jitters, she thought, dismissing it. She made no effort to go back into the crowded living room. No one had even noticed she'd disappeared, which was a blessing. This was the first time in days when she'd been alone, it seemed. At peace.

Until he stepped out of the shadows. "Running away?" Jake Wyczynski murmured.

He didn't come any closer, for which she could only be thankful, though she wasn't quite sure why.

He was marginally dressed up, in dark pants and an open-necked white shirt, but there was no missing the air of the wild, the exotic, that clung to him like the night breeze.

"Getting a breath of air," she said lightly. "I didn't realize you were here."

"I've been hiding out. This isn't my kind of thing, I'm afraid."

She turned and leaned against the stone balustrade, looking up at him. "Then why are you here?"

"I promised your godmother I'd give her a full report. If that means having to suffer through cocktail parties then so be it." He looked as if he'd rather be wrestling crocodiles than standing on the terrace of the Andersons' elegant house.

"Hey, don't hang around on my account. I absolve you of any obligation," she said coolly.

"The obligation isn't to you, sweetheart. It's to Louisa. I promised I'd witness your wedding and all the garbage leading up to it, and I won't go back on my promise even if it kills me."

"It's not going to," she said. "Though I might be tempted. I'll tell you what, I can always free you. The invitation is rescinded. You aren't invited. You can return to the wilds with a clear conscience."

"I think your mother might have something to say about that."

He was absolutely, annoyingly right. Her mother wouldn't tolerate such ill manners, especially toward the representative of one of her oldest friends. Susan sighed wearily. She would have liked nothing better than to get rid of him, though she couldn't figure out why he bothered her so much. In any case, she had no choice but to summon some semblance of courtesy. "All right," she said. "You can suffer as much as you want. Just don't expect me to make it any more bearable. I've got too much going on as it is."

She made the mistake of meeting his gaze. He really had extraordinary eyes, light blue in his deeply tanned face, and there was the strangest expression in them. It must have been a trick of the light.

He smiled wryly. "I'm not expecting anything but a week of utter boredom and then I can get the hell back to where I came from."

"And where did you come from?" she inquired politely.

"Here, there and everywhere. I'm a wanderer. A jack-of-all-trades. The last time I saw your godmother she was in Tanzania, about to climb Mount Kilimanjaro. I imagine the next time I run into her it'll be in Sri Lanka at a ruined temple, or maybe a deserted Incan city."

"How...completely irresponsible. Don't you need to make money, or are you independently wealthy?"

"No, I don't need to make money," he echoed in a cynical drawl. "I don't need to do much of anything I don't want to do. I get to live a life of complete freedom."

"And it isn't lonely?"

He paused, looking at her. Somehow, in the course

of a short conversation, they'd gone from polite to hostile, and she wasn't quite sure why. Only that she felt safer with the hostility. "Let me tell you, sweetheart, it seems a hell of a lot lonelier in the middle of that crowd of people—" he jerked his head toward the noisy living room "—than being alone on an African river."

She wanted to refute it, but the one thing she always prided herself on was her honesty. "You're right," she said abruptly.

He clearly hadn't expected her to admit as much. "Then why are you putting up with it?"

"It's expected. Edward enjoys it, and it helps his career. Did you meet Edward, by the way? I'll introduce you...." She started for the French doors, suddenly eager to get away, back to the crowds and the safety, when he caught her arm. His hand was rough, warm, strong on her forearm.

"I met Edward," he said. "I didn't like him."

She stared up at him, openmouthed, too astonished to pull free. "I beg your pardon? Everyone likes Edward."

"I don't. He's plastic. A complete and utter phony, more interested in his own reflection than you. Are you sure you want to spend the rest of your life married to such a jerk?"

Her momentary shock melted into fury. "Just who the hell do you think you are? It's none of your business who I marry. I don't even know you." Belatedly she yanked her arm free, then realized he hadn't even been holding her. Just resting his hand on her arm.

He shrugged, unimpressed. "I hate to see people screwing up their lives."

"Fine," she said. "Don't look." She started away from him, when his mocking drawl called her back.

"You didn't say whether you liked today's present?"

She paused by the door. "I don't know what it is."

"Wedding jewelry, from one of the nomadic tribes Louisa and her husband traveled with."

"Wedding jewelry? Where do you wear it?" she demanded.

He grinned. "Next to the skin, babe. If you and old Edward can't figure it out you can always come to me."

She slammed the door behind her.

Chapter Three

He watched her storm off, unwilling admiration warring with his definite annoyance. She was easily riled, which surprised him. He'd gathered from the people who'd known Susan Abbott all her life that she was an abnormally even-tempered young lady. Even Louisa had assured him that her unknown goddaughter had the temperament of a lamb.

Like a lamb to the slaughter, and realizing just how badly she was trapped, he thought. Maybe it was just nerves—he figured brides were supposed to be edgy. But anyone with half a brain could see that she and Edward Jeffries were no decent match. And while he had his doubts about Susan's serenity, he had no illusions about her intelligence.

She was heading straight for dear old Edward, and her fiancé was flashing his perfect smile at her, tucking her hand on his Armani-suited arm. Jake knew Armani when he saw it, despite his preferred life on the outskirts of civilization, and Edward wore it well.

Jake turned away, oddly bothered by the sight of

them, surrounded by their neighbors and well-wishers. The terrace was only a few feet off the ground—he had every intention of jumping down rather than making his way through the perfumed crush once more.

He'd thrown one leg over the stone balustrade when someone loomed up out of the shadows beneath him. "Are you stealing the Andersons' silver?" the man drawled, "or are you just making a quick getaway?"

Jake landed on the soft ground. The lights from the house spread out over the lawn, illuminating the middle-aged man who stood there watching him. "Who wants to know?"

"I'm not security, if that's what you're worried about. I couldn't care less if you ran off with everything Taylor Anderson owns. I'm just an uninvited guest."

"I thought everyone and his brother was invited to this shindig," Jake said bitterly. "Though I can't imagine why anyone would choose to go if they didn't have to."

"Well, since I'm a party crasher I obviously disagree with you," he said pleasantly.

"Not much of a party crasher if you're down here and the party's going on up there. Trust me, you're not missing much. The champagne is too warm and the food is too cold."

"I'm not particularly interested in eating. How are the happy couple?"

Jake snorted in derision. "Happy enough," he said. "After all, they're a match made in blue-blood heaven."

"So they are," the man said thoughtfully. He held out a hand. "I'm Alex Donovan, by the way. Outcast from blue-blood heaven."

"I never belonged in the first place," Jake said, shaking his hand. "Why don't you go on in? There are so damned many people they'd never notice an extra one."

"I don't need to get any closer. I prefer it this way." He glanced at Jake. "Are you a friend of Edward's?"

"No."

"Then you must be a friend of Susan's."

"Not particularly. I'm a friend of her godmother's, here under duress."

"Louisa? How extraordinary," Alex murmured. "I can't believe she'd turn up after all these years."

"She didn't."

"She was smart. I should have kept my distance, as well," he said. "Are you going back in there?"

"Not if my life depended on it."

"Then let me buy you a drink," Alex said.

"Why? A sudden longing for company?" Jake had survived a rough thirty-five years by never taking anything at face value. He'd also survived by using his instinct, and his instincts told him that though Alex Donovan might have some secrets, he was a decent man.

"No. I just want to find out anything you know about Susan Abbott."

"I don't know much. Why should you care, anyway?" For some reason he liked him. Better than almost anyone he'd met since he'd come to Connecticut.

Alex Donovan smiled wryly. "Because I haven't seen her in twenty-nine years, and she's my daughter."

"WELL, I THINK that was very successful, don't you?" Susan said breathlessly as she followed her mother into the house. "All the right people, excellent food, decent champagne."

"Mmm." Her mother made a noncommittal sound.

"Even Jake Whatsisname looked halfway presentable." She kicked off her flat shoes and sprawled on her mother's chintz sofa. She never wore heels around Edward—they were the same height, and while he'd never complained, she suspected he didn't like it when she towered over him. Unfortunately it put her at a disadvantage with Jake Wyczynski—he positively loomed over her and she would have given anything to be able to look him in the eye.

"Wyczynski, darling, and you know it," Mary said gently. "Actually I think he looked quite gorgeous, and so did every single one of your bridesmaids. Laura Hayden was practically drooling over him."

"Deb was worse." Susan stretched out her long legs, yawning. "I told her he was married, but I don't think even that discouraged her."

"Why on earth did you do that? He isn't, is he? I'm sure Louisa would have mentioned it."

Susan jerked her head up. "You've talked with her?"

"She sent me a little note, explaining about Jake and the wedding gifts. Not that I needed any explanation. Louisa can always be expected to do the unusual."

"What did she say about him?"

"Why do you care?"

Susan produced an airy shrug that should have managed to hide her momentary guilt. "Just curious. I'm not used to having Indiana Jones show up at my doorstep bearing gifts from my mysterious godmother."

"I think he looks more like that man in *The English Patient*."

"Before or after he was burned?" Susan drawled.

"And you haven't told me why you lied to Deb. She's between beaux right now, and there's no reason she shouldn't entertain herself with Jake. I think they'd make a lovely couple."

"It would be disastrous. Deb's much too vulnerable—"

"Deb Stover is entirely capable of taking care of herself. Are you sure you don't have another reason for scaring her off Jake? You seem far too interested in him."

"I'm not the slightest bit interested in him. I'm not someone out of a screwball comedy, about to run off with a mountain man on my wedding day."

"No, you're a nervous bride who's not absolutely convinced she's making the right decision."

The gently spoken words were like a slap in the face. Susan stared up at her mother in shock. "I'm thirty years old, mother. Edward is everything I've ever wanted in this life—security, comfort, friendship. We'll have a good life together."

"What about love? What about passion?"

"I saw where that got you. I can do very well without it, thank you very much. You've lived the past thirty years quite happily, and you didn't miss it at all."

"Who says?" Mary started toward the bedroom door, looking suddenly older than her fifty-nine years, and Susan stared at her in shock and guilt.

"You gave it up because of me," she said, stricken. "I just assumed you were happy, when all the time you were sacrificing—"

Mary whirled around. "Don't be silly, darling. I didn't make any sacrifices I didn't want to make. I didn't give up on love and passion for your sake. I just never found anyone I cared about. Not the way I cared about your father."

"Then why didn't you try to work it out with him?"

Mary shook her head. "That was in the past. No need to belabor it now. I just don't want to see you making the same mistakes I made."

"That's why I'm marrying Edward. I don't want to marry the wrong man like you did."

"Oh, Susan," she said gently. "I didn't marry the wrong man, sweetheart. My mistake was leaving him." She shut the door behind her with quiet firmness, and Susan sank back on the sofa.

It had never occurred to her that her mother might have regretted her choices. That her own choices might not be the wise, rational decisions she'd prided herself on.

And she couldn't rid herself of the feeling that her mother was lying to her, trying to spare her feelings. That she'd spent the past thirty years living like a nun for the sake of her ungrateful daughter.

She'd deny it, of course. Susan pushed herself off the sofa and headed for the kitchen, looking for something to calm her nerves. Prewedding jitters, of course. All brides had them. Doubts and second guesses were an occupational hazard. And the unexpected appearance of Jake Wyczynski didn't help things.

Though there was no particular reason why she should find him so unsettling. She'd seen dangerously good-looking men before and she considered herself impervious to their dubious appeal. But the fact of the matter was that this time, this man, was different.

Four more days until the wedding, and every single minute was crammed with things to do. She hadn't been sleeping well, even though she usually prided herself on being unflappable, and if she had any sense at all she'd head into the bedroom and go right to sleep.

However, she'd learned the hard way that sense and sleep had no connection whatsoever. And she knew that despite the bare five hours of intermittent sleep she'd had the night before, she was far from ready to go to bed.

She made as little noise as possible when she went to her room, stripping off the perfect little black dress and pulling on an ancient pair of jeans and an old sweatshirt, shoving her bare feet into a pair of sandals. She washed off the makeup, shoved her fingers through her short hair and headed out into the cool night air, taking in a deep breath. She'd been feeling oddly stifled all night long, surrounded by people and demands, and the quiet stillness was balm to her soul.

The streets were empty, quiet, as she set out at a leisurely pace, stretching her long legs. She had no particular destination in mind, but it came as no surprise to her when she ended up on Forrest Street, just down the block from Winnie's All-Night Café.

Winnie was long gone—the place was run by two transplanted yuppies who'd installed an espresso machine and served biscotti, but you could still find the best doughnuts and French fries in the world. Susan usually contented herself with a salad and latte, but tonight she was in need of comfort food.

She slid into a booth, ordered a huge, greasy cheeseburger and fries, washed down by a Coke, and leaned back, closing her eyes, as the sound of New-Age music drifted in the background. She hadn't eaten anything at the party tonight. She'd only nibbled at lunch—it was no wonder that she'd gotten overwrought. She had to remember to eat—there was no frilly, too-small wedding dress to starve herself into. Her doomed aunt Tallulah's satin wedding dress fit her frame perfectly—if she lost any weight it wouldn't hang as well, and there was hardly time to get it altered.

Anyway, she needed junk food tonight with a passion that would brook no denial. She smiled faintly. And her mother thought her devoid of passion. Not when it came to food.

She was halfway through her fries when something made her look up toward the door, in time to see Jake Wyczynski, his tall body shielding another man, the soft murmur of voices reaching to her booth. She ducked her head, hoping he wouldn't see her but simply follow his friend out, but luck was against her. The other man left, and Jake ambled toward her, with that sexy, graceful slouch that had become unaccountably annoying.

He slid into the other side of the booth without waiting for an invitation, and helped himself to one of her French fries.

"Now who would have thought I'd run into the ice princess at a sleazy all-night diner?" he said, leaning back against the cracked vinyl banquette. "This hardly seems like your kind of place."

"You don't know anything about me. What makes you think you're an expert on what my kind of place is? Some people head for a bar, I head for French fries when I need to—" She'd almost said "drown her sorrows." "When I need to think."

"What do you need to think about?" He took another fry. "Never mind, you're going to tell me it's none of my damned business."

"I'm not that rude."

"Not to most people, I've noticed. But with me you're able to rise to the occasion."

"You bring out the worst in me."

"Why?"

She closed her eyes briefly and sighed. "This is a crazy conversation. Go away, Jake. I have more important things on my mind."

"I like the way you say my name."

Her eyes flew open. "Don't!"

"Don't what?"

"Don't flirt with me. And don't deny that was what you were doing. I've got enough on my mind without that."

He reached for another French fry and popped it in his mouth. She had to admit he had a disturbingly sexy mouth. "What's on your mind, then? Cold feet? Having second thoughts about dear old Edward?"

"No," she said flatly. "Edward is everything I've ever wanted in life, and we'll have a wonderful life together. It's only natural to feel nervous when you're about to take such a major step in life."

"You don't take too many chances, do you?"

"Not if I can help it. I like security. Surprises disturb me."

He sighed. "You can't control life, Susan. It has a habit of throwing curve balls when you least expect it. You need to learn to duck or bat."

She liked the way he said her name, too, she thought dismally. "I was never very good at softball," she said. "I can simply refuse to play."

"Life is hardball. But you'll miss a lot if you're too scared to take chances."

"I'm not scared."

"Aren't you?" He reached for another French fry, and she glared at him.

"Take one more and you die," she said. "Order your own if you want fries."

"I'll take that as an invitation." He rose and went to the counter, and her eyes followed him with dubious fascination. She should be home in bed at this hour, not having a midnight rendezvous with a dangerous man. And there was no question about it, Jake Wyczynski was a dangerous man indeed, at least to Susan Abbott.

He slid back into the booth, a cup of coffee in his hand. Edward would have stayed put, snapping his well-manicured fingers until the harried waitress came to take his order.

"You can't find truly great French fries outside of this country and Canada. It could be what I miss most," he said.

"Every place in the world has McDonald's."

He laughed, a low, lazy laugh. "That's what you think. I keep away from big cities if I can help it."

"Where do you live? For that matter, who the hell are you?" she demanded, sliding over to the corner and curling her feet up underneath her. She'd given up fighting for the moment. She'd come to her haven, the one place where she was certain she wouldn't run into anyone she knew, and he was there. There were some things not worth fighting. An hour's conversation over coffee and French fries wouldn't do any harm. Besides, she was curious.

"I don't want to talk about me."

"Tough," she said sweetly. "What have you got to hide?"

"Unlike you, a hell of a lot."

"What makes you think I don't have anything to hide?" she demanded, oddly offended.

"You've lived a blameless life, haven't you? Straight As in the proper prep school, one of the seven sisters colleges, the perfect daughter, the best friend, the proper fiancée. Always doing and saying the right thing."

It shouldn't have wounded. She smiled tightly. "You're very astute."

"Except that I don't think that's what you really are. I think that beneath that polished, perfect exterior is wild woman trying to escape."

"Nope," she said. "There is no wild woman inside me. You're a romantic."

"Yes."

"So tell me how you know my godmother, who has to be the most elusive human being on this planet. Where do you live, and what do you do for a living? And don't brush me off with some glib answer. I'm curious. Consider it a gift of charity. I need to be distracted from the pressures of my wedding. Entertain me."

He toyed with his cup of coffee, and she looked at his hands. They were rough, scarred, tanned and oddly elegant as they encircled the thick mug. Good hands, gentle but strong.

"All right," he said. "Where do I live? Right now it's in an abandoned garage in the middle of your family's property. That'll be home for another week. Then I'll head to Spain, then on to East Africa, and then I'm not sure."

"You don't have a home?"

"Several, in fact. Nothing particularly elegant. The old farmhouse in Spain is probably in better shape than the other places, but that's because I spend more time there. A hunting cabin in the Northwest Territories of Canada. A tiny cattle ranch in Argentina. A truly disreputable house in Venice. A number of other places scattered throughout the world.''

"So instead of Indiana Jones you're really a jet-setting millionaire, traveling between your many homes?''

He laughed. "Nope. I don't like to be tied down. I have a knack for making money when I need it. Louisa says I'm the luckiest human being she knows, but I'm not so sure of that. I just have a certain ability to know what will work and what won't.''

"So you basically wander the world, making investments like some banker? It sounds boring.''

He laughed. "The last job I had was building bridges in East Africa. Trust me, it wasn't boring in the slightest.''

"How do you know Louisa?''

"She's my aunt. Married to my uncle Jack for forty-eight years, until he died in his sleep. Damned tame way for the old man to go, too.'' He sighed. "She's a character, your godmother. A holy terror, not afraid of anything or anyone, with the biggest heart and the deepest laugh.''

"She sounds like the stories I've heard of my aunt Tallulah,'' Susan said faintly.

"I imagine they've got a lot in common.''

"It's probably just as well she didn't come for the wedding. She'd be sorely disappointed in her god-child.''

"Why do you say that?''

"You've already pointed out what a good little girl

I am. Always doing and saying the right thing. Do you think someone like Louisa would appreciate such a boring little paragon?'' She couldn't keep the faint bitterness out of her voice.

"The thing about Louisa," Jake said in a soft voice, "is that she knows people. She'd see right through you to the woman beneath. I think she'd love you."

She jerked her head up, startled. "Why?"

"Because you have a fierce heart. You make me think of some fairy-tale princess, the whole world trapped inside you while you sleep."

"Don't start thinking you're going to awaken me with a kiss," she warned him, feeling a sudden knot in her stomach.

"Who's talking about kissing?" he replied lazily.

"I've got to go." She almost knocked her half-empty Coke over on the Formica counter in her haste to get away. She fumbled in her purse, and he reached out and put his hand over hers, stilling her agitated movements.

"My treat," he said. "It's the least Louisa would expect of me."

His hand was warm, big, strong, and she couldn't control the stray shiver that ran through her body. She jerked it away, rather than argue. "It's been nice talking to you, Mr. Wyczynski."

"Always polite," he murmured wryly. "You don't always have to come up with the polite lies, Susan."

"You haven't lived in civilized society recently. Polite lies are an important part of life."

"All right. How about you don't have to lie to me?"

She rose, staring at him, and she knew with sudden certainty that lying to Jake Wyczynski was more important than any of the small social lies the told daily. "I'd better get home and get to bed," she said nervously. "I've got the week from hell ahead of me."

Too late she realized how that sounded. "Not that I'm not happy and excited," she continued quickly. "I mean, what bride wouldn't be? It's just—"

"Go home, Susan," he said gently. "You can come up with excuses tomorrow.

He was wrong about her. She wasn't a coward, not usually. But at that moment she didn't have any fight left in her. With a faint, nervous shrug, she turned and ran.

Chapter Four

Susan didn't sleep well. The French fries, what few Jake hadn't eaten, sat in her stomach like a lump of lead. Every time she came close to drifting off, something would wake her up. The guest bed in her mother's house was brand-new, state-of-the-art and hard as a rock. Perfect for bones and muscles, but hell to get comfortable in, she thought, punching her pillow at a little past six.

At seven she gave up, staggering to the kitchen to make some fresh coffee. She caught a glimpse of her reflection in the mirror and shuddered. Her close-cropped hair stuck out all around her head, her face was pale except for the lavender circles around her eyes, and her mouth looked tight and drawn. The blushing bride looked like death warmed over, and if she didn't get some sleep in the next three days, Edward was going to see her coming down the aisle and bolt in the opposite direction.

It wasn't until she poured her second cup of black,

strong coffee that she realized the notion of Edward
running away filled her with profound relief.

"You're being an idiot," she said out loud. In-
decision wasn't her style, and now was a hell of a
bad time to change her mind. Edward was everything
she'd ever wanted. She certainly wasn't going to
back out now.

Grabbing a yellow, lined legal pad and a pencil,
she took her coffee out into the small backyard that
Mary had tended so lovingly over the years. Her
mother had done wonders with the tiny yard, the ordinary little house, but she deserved better, and Susan
had every intention of making sure she got it.

She drew a line down the center of the page, with
yes and no on either side. The reasons to marry Edward were easy enough. One, she loved him. Two,
the wedding was planned. Three, her mother loved
him. Four, this was her childhood dream come true.
Five, it would return the Abbotts to their rightful
place in Matchfield society. Six, she loved Edward.

On the no side, there was nothing. Apart from a
faint, indefinable sense of uneasiness that had to be
normal prenuptial nerves, she could think of absolutely no reason why she wouldn't want to marry
Edward Jeffries on Saturday. Well, apart from his
overwhelming mother.

It was all Jake Wyczynski's fault, and by exten-
sion, her mysterious godmother Louisa's fault as
well. Everything had been just fine until he showed
up, like some exotic jungle cat. Well, fine except for

Vivian Jeffries's horrible wedding dress, but she would have gladly worn that monstrosity in return for a little peace of mind.

She certainly didn't need someone like Jake second-guessing her well-thought-out decisions. Uncertainty was perfectly normal in a bride—perfectly normal in anyone approaching a major life change. Maybe she should call the doctor and see if she could get some tranquilizers. Maybe she should take up serious drinking. No, she couldn't do that. One of the few things she knew about her father was that he drank too much. It would be just her luck to inherit that tendency. Maybe she needed a honeymoon more than she realized.

Not that they were taking one. Susan was in the midst of changing jobs, so she was free, but Edward was a young man on the rise, and now was no time for him to be taking more than a couple of days off. The honeymoon would wait until they could do it right.

And Susan's brand-new passport sat in her top drawer, with no chance of it being used.

She was on her second cup of coffee when her mother joined her on the terrace, the newspaper in one hand and a box in the other. Susan looked up at her warily.

"What's that?"

"Another present from your godmother. Jake must have dropped it off early this morning."

"Oh, God," Susan groaned. "I don't want to deal with it."

"Susan! Louisa went to a great deal of trouble..."

"It's not because of Louisa," Susan said bitterly. "This week is complicated enough—I just don't need any more distractions."

"I'll put it away, then, and you can open it and the others afterward."

"That would be the intelligent thing to do," Susan said. "And I've always been such a thoughtful, intelligent human being."

"So you have," Mary said, dumping the present in her lap. "Are you going to open it or am I?"

Susan tore the wrappings away, exposing a beautiful old leather box tied with thongs. She opened it, staring down into the contents in consternation.

"Well, what is it?" her mother demanded. "Some bizarre form of birth control? Camel jerky? I wouldn't put anything past Louisa."

Slowly Susan lifted the various items from the box and set them on the glass-topped table in front of her. An ancient passport, dated in the nineteen fifties, the photo torn away, the name barely readable except for the "Louisa," every page of it stamped and visa'd with destinations and locales from every continent. There were photographs of various women from long ago, including one Susan recognized as Amelia Earhart and another she suspected was the famous Victorian traveler, Lady Hester Stanhope.

The final item was an antique travel diary, bound in embossed leather. Empty, waiting to be filled.

"How very interesting," Mary said mildly from over her shoulder.

Susan set the items back in the leather box with care. "Obviously my godmother doesn't know much about me," she said in a light voice. "I'm a homebody, not a world traveler. I've never even been out of the country."

"You used to have travel posters all over your walls when you were a teenager," Mary reminded her. "I remember you telling me that your life's dream was to see Venice."

"People change."

"So you don't want to see Venice?"

"I will sooner or later," she said, strangely uncertain of any such thing. "In the meantime, I need to put a stop to these presents." She rose, pushing the box away from her.

"I told you, I can simply put them away...."

"I don't have the willpower. Jake will simply have to hold on to the rest, assuming there are still more to come, until after I'm married. I can deal with this."

"And how are you going to find him?"

"I think I know where he's staying," Susan said.

"I don't know if that's a wise idea. You seem to react very strongly to Jake Wyczynski. I've never seen you get so upset. It's quite unlike you. Maybe I should deal with it."

"No!" Susan said sharply. "I'm not a complete coward. It's my problem and I'll deal with it. The man just gets on my nerves."

"I never said you were a coward, Susan. I just worry about you."

She kissed her mother briskly on one cheek. "Don't worry. I have everything under control. I always do."

"Yes," said Mary, sounding less than happy with the notion. "You always do."

JAKE SLEPT LATE, dragging himself out of his sleeping bag sometime in the early afternoon. He figured he might as well try to stay on African time rather than try to adjust for one short week. Besides, most of the things he was supposed to attend were at night, anyway, when he'd just be waking up.

He was on his second cup of coffee when he heard someone outside the old garage. He froze, definitely not in the mood for visitors, or anyone he'd have to justify his presence to. He had every right and permission to be camping there, but he preferred not sharing that information with the world.

Whoever was outside knew exactly where they were going. He heard measured footsteps on the rickety stairs, and he sighed, wondering whether he was going to be facing an irate groundskeeper or the local police.

He would have preferred either of those two unpleasant possibilities to Susan Abbott, her tall, slim body silhouetted in the doorway in the afternoon light.

"I thought I'd find you here," she said with a trace of smugness.

He didn't move. He was only wearing an old pair of cutoff jeans, no shirt or shoes, but he was damned if he was going to cover himself up. After all, he hadn't invited her—she was just going to have to put up with his lack of attire.

"I wasn't trying to be mysterious," he said mildly.

She walked into the room, looking around curiously. She was dressed casually, in a pair of faded jeans and a T-shirt, and he noticed dismally that he liked her breasts. It came as no surprise, but in her formal clothes he'd been able to keep his mind off them. He seldom found elegantly dressed women attractive. Put them in T-shirts or flannel and his hormones were far more likely to surge.

"You do your absolute best to be as mysterious as possible," she corrected him gently. "Do you have any more of that coffee?"

"It's instant," he warned her.

She wrinkled her nose. "I would have thought you had higher standards."

"I'm flexible. I'll take my caffeine any way I can get it. That's the trick to enjoying life, you know. Savor the fresh-ground beans when you can, make do with instant if there's no alternative."

"Thank you for that scintillating view of life," Susan said. She crossed the room, her sneakers making little noise on the old floor. "I have a favor to ask of you."

He allowed himself a slow, tantalizing grin. "Anything you want, babe."

She shuddered visibly. "Don't call me babe," she said in that patented frosty tone of hers.

"Is that all? I can always come up with sweetheart, honey, baby-cakes—"

"If you call me baby-cakes I'll cut your throat."

"It's been tried."

He'd managed to startle her. "You're not serious!"

"Absolutely. I ran afoul of some street bandits in Alexandria a few years back and still have the scars to prove it. I'm harder to kill than you might think. But I doubt you find it surprising that someone would want to kill me."

"I can sympathize," she said drily.

"So what's the favor?"

"Could you put on a shirt? I'm not used to having conversations with men who are barely dressed."

"No," he said. She wouldn't look at his face, she wouldn't look at his chest, she kept her gaze centered somewhere over his left shoulder. He was half tempted to turn and see whether Godzilla was creeping up behind him. "Anything else?"

"You're not very accommodating, are you? Is it just me, or are you this contrary with everyone?"

"I can be extremely accommodating when it counts," he murmured. "And I do admit, you bring out a certain contrary streak in me. So apart from putting on a shirt, what do you want me to do for you?''

"Stop bringing me presents.''

He shook his head. "No can do. I promised Louisa, and I always keep my promises.''

"Well, leave them in my mother's garage where I don't have to see them. They upset me.''

"Upset you? Why should they? Louisa went to a great deal of trouble, planning things for each day. Don't you think it's a little self-absorbed of you to simply reject them?''

"I'm allowed to be self-absorbed, I'm the damned bride!'' she said.

He rose. "Calm down, princess. You've got the worst case of bridal jitters I've ever seen. Are you absolutely sure you're doing the right thing?''

It didn't take a psychic to figure out she wasn't sure of any such thing. "Of course I'm sure. I just don't need you and your gifts distracting me.''

"I'm a distraction? How so?''

She glared at him, standing her ground as he approached her, tilting her head back to look at him out of those flinty green eyes. He had a weakness for tall women, and Susan Abbott was a suitably strapping wench. It was probably something as simple as that—he was attracted to the sheer size of her, and it made him randy.

He stopped within inches of her, curious to see whether she'd back away. She took a deep, shuddering breath but didn't move, squaring her shoulders. "Go away, Jake," she said in a deceptively firm voice. "Please."

It would be the worst mistake of his life if he touched her. He was still haunted by the feel of her skin beneath his hand when he'd caught her wrist last night. He still dreamed about the creamy smoothness of her back when he'd ripped the wedding dress off her. But he knew perfectly well he was more likely to regret the things he didn't do than the things he did.

He slid his hand underneath her short cropped hair, cupping her slender neck. She made a choking sound, but she didn't pull away from him. She simply looked at him out of huge, wary eyes, her soft, pale lips parted. He could feel the pulse pounding in her neck, and he moved closer still, crowding her, so that their bodies almost touched.

"You can't run away from everything you're afraid of," he whispered.

"I'm not," she said in a raw voice. "I just want you to go away."

"Tell me why I should?"

"Because I'm asking you, as a favor. I know you don't owe me any favors, but maybe you could consider it a gesture of goodwill."

"Why do you want me to go away? Why do I disturb you?"

She wasn't going to answer, and he knew it.

"Maybe I should show you," he said finally. And he put his mouth against hers.

She could have broken free quite easily—they both knew it. He held her lightly, one hand cupping her neck, the other at her waist, but she made no effort to escape. She simply held very still as he kissed her, slowly, tasting her lips and nothing more.

He felt her strong hands on his shoulders, cool against his hot flesh. They tightened for a moment, clinging to him, and desire surged through him with such powerful force that he shook. He pulled her closer against him, so that her body was plastered up against his nearly nude one, so that she could feel how hard he was, how much he wanted her. She tasted of fresh strawberries and coffee, and he wanted more, he wanted to taste every part of her, he wanted to strip off her clothes and drag her over to that narrow, sagging bed.

"Open your mouth," he whispered against her soft lips.

Her eyes shot open, and she jerked away from him so fast he couldn't even attempt to hold on to her. Even though he wanted to. Before he realized it she was halfway across the room, and he was hard as a rock and freezing cold.

She didn't look back. She ran as if she were being chased by a pack of wild pigs, and he was half-afraid she'd tumble down the rickety side steps in her hurry to get away from him. By the time he moved over to the window she was disappearing into the woods, down a different path than he was used to. The early-summer greenery swallowed her up, and she was gone, as if she'd never been there.

He began to swear. Swearing was one of his many talents—he could curse in more than twenty languages, usually with an inventiveness that impressed men around the world. He rose to new heights in the moments after Susan Abbott ran away from him, and it was only a shame that no one was there to appreciate his colorful invective.

He was covered in a cold sweat, he was as hard as a lust-crazed teenage boy, and worse than that, he'd betrayed Louisa. His uncle's wife had been like a second mother to him, and he'd always considered it an honor to perform the rare, small tasks she'd asked of him.

Coming to America and being stuck here for a week at a society wedding was no small task, of course, but he'd agreed to it willingly enough. But she hadn't expected him to end up sabotaging her goddaughter's peace of mind. And maybe even the wedding itself.

And then there was Alex Donovan. He'd ended up going to Winnie's Diner instead of a bar, and he'd sat nursing a cup of coffee while Donovan tried to find out anything he knew about his daughter. It wasn't Jake's nature to pry—he'd spent too many years in cultures where privacy was of utmost importance—but Donovan had been wryly informative, making no excuses. His marriage to Mary Abbott had ended before Susan could even remember him, and his ex-wife and her family had made it clear he wasn't welcome.

There was something more to it than that, but Jake wasn't about to push it. So he told Donovan about his daughter, trying to keep it as neutral as possible, until Donovan's sharp green eyes, a match to his daughter's, looked at him shrewdly and he said, "You're in love with her."

He'd laughed. "And you're out of your mind. For one thing, I don't even know her. For another, she's not my type. And for a third, she's about to marry Mr. Perfect."

"My mistake," Donovan said softly. Clearly, annoyingly, unconvinced.

He was a man who'd abandoned his daughter for all her young life, for whatever reasons he might have. But Jake had the unpleasant suspicion that he wouldn't stand by and abandon her now, particularly if he saw someone intent on screwing up her life.

Hell, Susan Abbott was screwing up her life quite nicely without any help from him. If he could just keep his hands to himself, keep his damned mouth shut then she could go ahead and make her own mistakes, and he could go back to Louisa with a clear conscience and a full report.

Maybe she was right, maybe he should just go away. He could drop off the other two presents with Susan's mother and make a quick getaway, and chances were he could avoid ever seeing her again.

Or by the time he did, his hormones and his brain would be back in working order, and he'd see her as she would then be: an overbred, overeducated Connecticut matron with a yuppie husband, two kids and a van.

He didn't like the idea of her having Edward's kids, but it was none of his damned business. Louisa would be disappointed in him if he ran away, but she'd be a hell of a lot more upset if he screwed up Susan Abbott's wedding.

He was going to get the hell out of there, as fast as he could.

But first he was going to find the coldest body of water he could find and jump in. And maybe then he'd stop thinking about Susan Abbott's mouth.

Chapter Five

She wasn't used to running away, but Susan raced through the tangle of early-summer growth that strangled the access to the deserted garage, oblivious to the scratching branches and the uneven footing on the neglected path. Her mouth burned, her skin burned, and she wanted, needed, to run away and hide.

She'd left her car parked by the edge of Matchfield Commons, and she fumbled with her keys, her hands shaking. It was early afternoon on a weekday—the streets were empty, which was a damned good thing, she thought, shoving her hair out of her face. She was driving like a maniac, with nothing more important than making it back to her mother's house and the privacy of the guest bedroom. She'd had too little sleep, too much stress. A few hours of quiet, maybe a nap, would put it all in perspective.

She peeled into the driveway, much too fast, breathing a sigh of relief when she saw her mother's Saturn was gone. She wasn't in the mood to answer any questions at the moment, and her mother had the unfortunate gift of seeing through most of Susan's most tactful evasions.

She slammed the door behind her and stared at her reflection in the mirror. It was a damned good thing Mary was out. Susan Abbott looked as if she'd been most thoroughly kissed.

As she had. She didn't remember being that shaken by another man's mouth in years. Maybe in her entire life. Edward wasn't much for kissing—Susan suspected that deep down he considered it a bit unsanitary.

Her face felt tender from the scratch of Jake's unshaven face. Edward didn't have that heavy a beard, and yet he still shaved twice a day. She touched the faint red mark by her mouth, her fingers delicate, curious. In truth, it hadn't even been that much of a kiss. She'd panicked before he could deepen it, which was a good thing. She had already been close to succumbing to the erotic pressure of his mouth against hers. If he'd used his tongue she probably would have dragged him over to the bed she'd been far too aware of.

She pushed away from the mirror in disgust, shaking her head. What in God's name had come over her? She'd never been prey to irrational, surging hormones, she'd never been emotional, irresponsible, filled with the kind of aching desire better suited to a *Titanic* addict.

She heard the phone ring, but she ignored it. It

was probably something she'd forgotten, one of those thousands of questions that only the bride could answer. They could leave a message and Mary would call them back.

The answering machine clicked on, and Susan started nervously as Edward's disembodied voice floated toward her from the answering machine. "Susan, dear, are you there? I'm afraid I'm going to have to stay in the city tonight, but I'll need you to take care of a few things. Have you got a pencil? There's my dry cleaning at Cecil's French Laundry on Dugan Street, and the jeweler told me the gifts for the ushers are in. And if you could possibly..."

She had her hand out to pick up the receiver, wanting, needing to remember why she was marrying him. But she couldn't move. She just stood there listening to the list of errands as they sailed right past her consciousness.

She was still standing there, five minutes later, when she heard someone drive up the driveway. Her immediate reaction was flight, out the kitchen door, but the backyard was a cul-de-sac, and there would be no escape. Besides, what did she have to escape from? As far as she knew Jake Wyczynski had no car—he wouldn't be able to follow her that quickly and finish what he started.

And Edward was still in the city—she was safe from him, as well. And she wasn't going to even consider why she was suddenly considering Edward to be as big a threat to her peace of mind as Jake.

It was probably just a delivery company with more of the interminable wedding gifts. Susan liked crystal and silver as well as anyone, but she couldn't really see centering her life around them. She'd simply pile the latest boxes in the garage and let Edward have the joy of opening them.

She swung open the front door, then stopped. It was no brown-shorts-clad UPS hunk but a tall, older man. He looked beyond surprised to see her standing at the door, he looked frankly appalled.

"May I help you?" Susan managed to be deceptively polite. She wasn't in the mood for religious fanatics or vacuum cleaner salesmen, though this man didn't actually look like either. He looked vaguely familiar, and Susan knew she must have met him at some point in her life.

"Er...is Mary Abbott home?"

"Sorry, she's out at the moment. I'm her daughter. May I give her a message?"

A faint, reluctant smile formed at his mouth. "'May you?'" he echoed. "She brought you up well."

Susan shrugged. "She did, as a matter of fact. Are you a friend of hers?"

"An old acquaintance. I should have called instead of just showing up, but I was in the neighborhood and I stopped by on a whim. I'll call next time."

He seemed to want to get away from her, back to the anonymous dark car he'd left parked in the driveway. And for some reason, despite her earlier desperate need for solitude, she didn't want to let him escape.

She followed him out into the driveway. "You could come in and wait for her," she suggested, wondering if she were out of her mind. A moment ago she'd been desperate for solitude. "I'm sure she won't be long—"

"No!" He sounded surprisingly vehement, and then he softened it with an oddly familiar smile. "I wouldn't think of intruding. I'll come back."

Something wasn't adding up, and Susan's instincts were infallible. "Who are you?" she demanded abruptly as he reached his sedan.

"Who am I?" he echoed, startled, his hand on the door.

"Are you the police? FBI?"

"God, no. Why would you think such a thing?" He looked seriously bewildered.

"The bland rental car, the dark suit, the mysterious manner," she said. "Of course, you aren't wearing dark glasses and you're not traveling in pairs, but still…"

"Maybe my partner is circling around the back."

She suddenly realized how absurd the whole thing was. "Sorry," she said. "I haven't had enough sleep, and my imagination is going haywire."

"You don't have any reason to think the police or the FBI would be coming around, do you?" He suddenly looked worried, disproportionately so.

She shook her head. "No, my mother and I live

very ordinary lives. It would make things more interesting if they did," she said. "So who are you?"

"Just tell your mother Bill came by. I'll be in touch."

She stood in the yard, watching as he drove away. Odd, he didn't look like a Bill. She racked her brain for any of the Williams her mother might have mentioned over the years, but the tall, older man didn't fit any of them. She'd seen him before, she knew she had, but she couldn't place him no matter how hard she tried.

She headed back into the house. It was midafternoon, and if she was going to accomplish any of Edward's list of tasks she needed to get moving.

But she knew perfectly well she wasn't going to do anything of the kind. She was going to have a very tall glass of iced tea, stuff some carbohydrates in her mouth and take a long, long nap. At least it was a relatively quiet night in this wedding week— she and her mother were supposed to go out for drinks, but it would be simple enough to cry off.

She was in the kitchen, mixing her iced tea and humming under her breath, a tuneless little hum. She didn't particularly feel like singing, but she couldn't get the song out of her mind.

She dropped several ice cubes in the tall glass of tea and brought it to her lips as the song danced through her mind. It was an old show tune, one that used to make her mother cry. Something about an ordinary guy....

The glass shattered at her feet, drenching her legs with iced tea, but she was frozen in place. The song was "Bill," from *Showboat,* and it had been her parents' special song for the short time when they'd been happy together. So special that Mary Abbott had called her husband Bill instead of Alex.

She cleaned up the mess in a daze, her brain simply shutting down. She wasn't going to think about the familiar/unfamiliar man who'd come by; she wasn't going to think about Jake Wyczynski's mouth; she wasn't going to think about all the things that Edward wanted her to do. She was going to her bedroom, and if everyone was extremely lucky she'd get up by her wedding day. But she was making no guarantees.

She closed and locked the door behind her, pulled the shades, stripping off the tea-stained clothes and dumping them in a pile. Her doomed aunt's wedding dress hung over the closet door, a reminder of all that lay ahead of her. Right now she was feeling just as doomed as poor Tallulah had been. Maybe she was crazy to wear that dress.

On impulse she pulled it off the padded hanger and slipped it over her head. It slid down her body in a shimmer of satin, settling around her like a caress.

She stared at her reflection in the mirror. The short-cropped, honey-blond hair, the high cheekbones, the green eyes stared back at her, familiar as always. And then the image shifted and melted, and for a moment she was looking at a different reflection, wavery, as if through candlelight. The woman in the mirror had a cloud of chestnut curls tumbling to her shoulders, huge brown eyes and a full, red-painted mouth. Her body was softer, less muscular, more rounded. She blinked, and the image vanished, and it was Susan again, biting her pale lips, staring at her reflection.

"You're out of your freaking mind, Abbott," she said out loud. "You kiss a stranger you barely know, much less like, you start imagining your long-lost father showing up at your doorstep, and now you're having hallucinations. Get a grip, woman!"

She glared at her reflection, daring it to shift again, but it stayed the way it was, a tall, frustrated bride in a beautiful dress who didn't know what in the world she really wanted.

The reflection shimmered again, suddenly, like a funhouse mirror, and the other woman was back, with her mane of dark hair, her saucy dark eyes, and her lipsticked mouth curving in a naughty smile. She looked like a movie star from the forties—a cross between Rita Hayworth and Ava Gardner. Susan reached out a tentative hand toward the strange reflection, and the woman in the mirror reached for her. But it wasn't Susan's hand. This hand had nail polish, and the biggest diamond she'd ever seen in her life, glittering through the wavering glass, sparkling.

A shaft of light speared through the room, sending

rainbows of light dancing around the room as if shot from a crazed prism.

Everything went black. Still and dark and black. And Susan was gone.

Part Two—Tallulah

Chapter Six

The bed was soft, cradling her body. In fact, it was too soft, which surprised Susan. Her mother had replaced the guest room bed before the wedding, and she'd bought one of those new orthopedic mattresses that were supposed to be so good for you but actually felt like you were sleeping on bricks.

It didn't matter. All that mattered was that she was sleeping, for the first time in what seemed like weeks. She knew she was asleep, knew it wouldn't take much to wake up, but she made the conscious decision to nestle into the bed and sink deeper and deeper into the gloriously welcome comfort of sleep.

She could feel the heavy satin of the wedding dress wrapped around her body, and she knew she should at least stagger out of bed and strip it off before it got hopelessly crushed. Mary would have a hissy fit if she saw Susan taking a nap in her aunt Tallulah's wedding dress.

But if she got up there and took off the dress there was no guarantee she'd get back to sleep in the next few hours, or even in this lifetime. No, she'd take the sleep when she could get it and deal with creased satin later.

It was quiet in the bedroom. A soft breeze was blowing across her body, which was another surprise. She'd left the central air-conditioning on, and the windows in her bedroom were locked.

It didn't matter, she reminded herself. Sleep. She mentally crooned the order like a hypnotist in a bad movie, and her body melted into the too-soft mattress.

And then her nose wrinkled in sudden dismay. The sheets beneath her smelled of cigarette smoke. So did the warm, fresh air around her. It smelled as if she were lying in a giant ashtray.

Sleep was gone, effectively banished, and she opened her eyes. It was dark in the room, the only light coming from the two double-hung windows that stood open against the twilight sky. She must have slept for hours—it was no wonder she felt dizzy, disoriented.

She sat up, blinking slightly, and rubbed a hand across her face. Her skin felt strange, hot and damp, and her mouth was covered in lipstick. Odd—she seldom wore lipstick, and she certainly hadn't put any on today. And if she had, Jake Wyczynski would have kissed it off her.

She didn't want to think about that. She didn't want to think about anything at all. She needed to see what she had to do to salvage the wedding dress.

She could hear the sound of voices in the distance, which surprised her. Her mother must have returned and brought someone with her. She could only hope and pray it wasn't Jake—she didn't think she could face him right now.

Whoever it was, they needed to leave. She had to ask her mother about the mysterious man who'd shown up at the front door calling himself "Bill."

She slid her legs over the side of the bed and tried to stand up, only to go sprawling on her face in the darkness. The bed was a good five inches higher than she'd anticipated.

She scrambled to her feet immediately, slightly shaken from her encounter with the bare wood floor. And then she froze.

The double bed in her mother's guest room was much closer to the floor than this one, and the entire house had discreet wall-to-wall carpeting. There wasn't a bare patch of wood anywhere in her place, thanks to the previous tenants, and while Mary bemoaned the lack of wooden floors, she couldn't bring herself to get rid of perfectly good carpeting, especially with money being tight.

She wasn't alone in the room. Someone was sitting by the window, in the shadows, the only sign the faint glow of his cigarette.

"Who the hell are you?" she demanded. "And what are you doing in my room? And why are you smoking—my mother doesn't allow smoking in the house...." Her voice trailed off in horror. It hadn't sounded like her voice at all. It was lower, huskier, sexier sounding. She must have picked up a cold from those damned open windows. Or hay fever.

"Don't get your knickers in a twist, Lou," a man's voice drifted from the corner. "I needed to talk to you in private, and I figured this might be my only chance without half your family wandering in and interrupting us. And just because your mother uses a silver cigarette holder doesn't mean she doesn't smoke almost a pack a day."

The cigarette went flying out the window, the red tip arcing against the darkness. "But if it offends you so much I can do without. I've practically given them up, anyway."

She took a tentative step toward him, peering in the darkness. All she could make out was a shadowy figure, definitely masculine, slightly familiar. A frisson of horror ran through her.

"That's not you, Jake, is it?" she demanded. "You have a hell of a lot of nerve coming in here uninvited."

"Jack, sweetheart, not Jake. You've only known me most of your life, why should I expect you to get my name right?" he said in a lazy drawl. "Are you going to come over here and talk to me before your sister comes barging in here?"

"I don't have a sister."

"That'll come as news to her and your parents."

"I don't have parents, either. Just my mother," she said stubbornly, refusing to consider the stranger who'd shown up at Mary's door just a few short hours ago.

"Fine," the man said. "I'm not going to argue with you about it. Are you going to listen to me or not?"

Susan didn't move. She felt a nervous, tickling sensation at the back of her neck, and she put her hand up, under the thick mane of curls. And then froze. She didn't have a thick mane of curls. She had short hair.

"Turn on the light," she said in an urgent, husky voice. A voice she didn't recognize.

The man in the corner moved, and a moment later a dim-watted bulb sent forth a pool of light into the strange room.

Be calm, she told herself. Don't panic, don't scream. There's a logical explanation for all of this.

She looked down at the wedding dress she'd put on such a short time ago. It was the same dress, slightly crumpled from her nap, but still skimming her body and reaching to her toes. Except that there were breasts in the way.

She clutched her chest. "What are these?" They felt real, warm and wrapped in a formidable bra. She yanked open the neckline and looked down. They were breasts all right, entrapped in a white foundation garment that looked downright medieval.

"I think they're boobs, Lou," the man named Jack said lazily. "You've had 'em since you were twelve."

She jerked her head up to stare at the stranger sitting in her bedroom. No, not her bedroom, a stranger's bedroom, smelling of stale cigarettes and Chanel Number Five. "What in God's name is going on?" she whispered. "Who the hell are you? And why are you calling me Lou?"

The man in her room gave her an inimical look. He had short, dark hair, pushed straight back from a tanned, angular face, and he was dressed in a rumpled suit, his tie unknotted and loosened around his neck. "I beg your pardon, Tallulah," he said, not bothering to hide his mockery. "Or should I say 'Miss Abbott'? And you know perfectly well who I am."

She took a step closer, then halted. "Humor me," the husky voice came from somewhere beneath those unfamiliar breasts.

"I'm Jack McGowan, Jimmy's brother, as you damned well know."

"Who's Jimmy?"

"If you're trying to tick me off you're doing a good job of it," he growled, reaching for his pack of cigarettes. "Jimmy's my kid brother. The boy you were going to marry. The war hero. The dead war hero."

"You're out of your mind," she said faintly.

He rose, obscuring the unfamiliar window, and he was very tall in the dim light. "You're the one who's acting like she's got a screw loose. Listen, Lou, you can't marry Ned Marsden, and you know it. The guy's no good, and I've got proof...."

"What are you talking about?"

With no more than a cursory knock the bedroom door flew open, and a child streaked in, stopping short in the middle of the room. "Hey, Lou," she said. "What's Jack doing here?"

The cynical, disapproving expression faded from Jack McGowan's face as he smiled down at the little girl, and he was suddenly, shockingly handsome. "How's my best sweetheart?"

"I'm not your best sweetheart, Jack," she said severely. "Lou is, though she won't admit it."

"What's going on?" Susan demanded weakly, one last time.

The girl looked up at her out of strangely familiar eyes. "What's wrong with her?" she demanded.

"Your sister seems to have developed a convenient form of temporary amnesia, probably to avoid making the worst mistake of her life."

"Don't be stupid, Lou," the girl said. "If you don't want to marry Neddie just tell him so. I don't like him, anyway—I think Daddy's the only one who really approves of him. You've got almost three days till the wedding—you can always call it off."

"Edward," she said dazedly. "I'm marrying Edward in three days."

"She's gotten very formal all of a sudden," Jack said. "She wants to be called Tallulah rather than Lou, so I guess Edward rather than Neddie is only logical. C'mon, squirt, let's leave the blushing bride alone, and maybe she'll remember the mess she's making of her life.''

"Wait!" Susan cried, as the two of them headed for the door, the tall, tall man and the child. The little girl turned around and looked at her out of Mary Abbott's blue eyes.

"What's wrong, Lou?" she demanded, looking worried.

She staggered back a few steps, until she came up against the high, unfamiliar bed. She sank down, dropping her head, and saw the dark curls veil her face.

"I'll be fine," she said in her strange voice. "Just give me a couple of minutes."

"Do you want me to send Mummy up?"

"No!"

"I don't blame you. Mummy's not very motherly, is she? I'll tell them you might not be down for dinner, and I'll see if Hattie can sneak you something later."

She looked up. The man stood silhouetted in the doorway, looking at her strangely. Somewhere in the distance she heard Frank Sinatra singing. She shivered in the warm air.

"Just give me a few minutes," she begged in that unfamiliar, sultry voice. "I'll be fine."

She heard their voices trail off behind the closed door, but she didn't move, standing completely still in the darkened bedroom, afraid, when she had always done her best to fight her fears. She took a deep, steadying breath and touched her hair again. The long flowing curls that didn't belong to her.

She pushed herself away from the bed and moved to the dressing table with its triptych mirror. There were two tall lamps on either side, and she sat down on the bench and switched them on, lifting her head to stare at her reflection without flinching.

The woman in the mirror looked a little simpleminded from shock, Susan thought wryly. And who wouldn't, facing a reflection that was completely foreign.

Well, not completely. She'd seen that face, that body in the mirror in her mother's house in Connecticut. And she'd seen that face, that body in one of the few old photographs her mother possessed of her long-dead sister.

The woman in the mirror was Tallulah Abbott. The woman whose body was encasing Susan's soul was Tallulah Abbott. Three days before her wedding day. Three days before her death.

Susan slammed down the panic that suddenly swelled into her throat. Maybe if she screamed she'd wake up, or maybe if she screamed all those people would come running again, and she'd have to come up with some sort of excuse. It had to be some crazy dream, brought on by the stress of the past few weeks, topped off by the appearance of Jake Wyczynski and the stranger who might possibly be her father. She was having the mother of all nightmares, and there was nothing to worry about.

She knew about dreams. How they mirrored the deeper concerns of everyday life. How they could teach you a lesson you were unwilling to learn during the day. No dream ever killed you, no matter how bizarre.

She could survive this dream in all its strangeness. She might wake up in a second, or it might take days. But panic would only make things worse.

She looked up at her reflection once more, taking a moment to enjoy it. She really did look like a cross between Ava Gardner and Rita Hayworth. The rich dark curls tumbled to her shoulders, her eyebrows were delicately plucked over huge, vibrant eyes, her nose was small and narrow, her mouth painted a lush crimson. For the first time in her life she was astonishingly beautiful, and she might as well enjoy it.

She rose and pulled off the wedding dress. It fitted more tightly than when she'd put it on, and she loosened the satin lacing in the front to get it off.

Her underwear was absurd. She had to be at least a thirty-six-C bra size, when she'd never been much more than a thirty-four A. She was more rounded, but still not in need of the thick rubber girdle that encircled her hips and held up the dark stockings.

She was about to peel off the girdle when she saw the maroon dress lying across a chair. It didn't take a rocket scientist to figure out she was supposed to wear that dress, but she wasn't ready to do that.

Wasn't certain she was ready to accept this dream, or nightmare.

Instead she found a chenille bathrobe hanging inside the closet door and she pulled it around her, oddly chilled in the warm air. She went over to the window to close it and then stopped, looking out over the wide, curving driveway.

She was at the old Abbott mansion. Where else would she be—that was where Tallulah and Mary had grown up, where Tallulah had lived before she married. Her grandparents had been forced to sell it in the fifties, and a decade later it had been struck by lightning and burned to the ground. All that remained was the garage that she could see to her right. The garage where Jake Wyczynski had kissed her.

It was a warm June night, and still Susan felt goose bumps crawling on her arms. Tallulah must have been a June bride as Susan was planning to be. For some reason it seemed unutterably sad to die in June.

She heard the door open once more, and she whirled around, only to see little Mary Abbott sneak inside, shutting the door quietly behind her.

"What's wrong with you, Lou?" she demanded. "Mummy and Daddy would have a fit if they knew you had a man in your bedroom. Particularly *that* man. Mummy's already half-tight, and Daddy's furious, demanding to know when you're coming down. Neddie doesn't look any too happy either."

"Half-tight?" Susan echoed, picking up on one small thing amidst Mary's spate of words.

"Smashed. Loaded. Bombed. She's been drinking. You know how she gets."

"Is it my fault?" Susan found herself asking. The question, the instinct was automatic and had nothing to do with Susan Abbott.

"Naaaah," Mary said with a precocious shrug. "Mummy dear will use any excuse. She'll get drunk tonight, she'll have a hangover tomorrow, and then she'll behave through the rest of the wedding. She probably won't go on another bender for at least a month. By then you'll be long gone."

"I hope so," Susan muttered, mainly to herself. "But what about you?"

Mary shrugged. "I keep out of her way when she gets like this. Don't worry about me, Lou. I'm good at taking care of myself. You taught me that."

Susan looked at the child who would one day be her mother. Mary Abbott had always seemed serene, able to weather the storms of life with surprising equanimity. She'd obviously learned it young.

"You said Ned Marsden is downstairs?"

"Do you know any other Neddie? He's over here every night. He wouldn't like it if he knew Jack was hanging around. He was always jealous of Jimmy, you know."

Susan took a deep breath. "Jimmy," she echoed. The dead war hero.

For a moment Mary looked preternaturally old,

worried and maternal. "What's wrong with you, Lou? And why haven't you dressed for dinner? You know Neddie's got an even worse temper than Daddy, and he's expecting you."

"I don't suppose you could convince them I wasn't feeling well," Susan suggested weakly.

"Not without having all of them troop up here to check on you. Why don't you tell me what's wrong and I'll see what I can do to fix it."

"You're nine years old. What can you do?"

"Well, at least you remember that much," Mary said. "You had me worried for a moment. Jack told me you were acting like you'd never seen him before in your life, but I figured he was making things up. He's a writer, after all, even if it's supposed to be the truth, Daddy says most journalists are born liars."

"He's a journalist?"

Mary came up to her and placed her small hands on Susan's larger ones. Foreign ones, with a big, gaudy diamond ring and nail polish. "What's wrong with you, Lou?" she asked quietly.

Susan looked at the little girl who seemed to be both her sister and her mother, and she didn't even hesitate.

"I'm not Tallulah."

Chapter Seven

Mary Abbott blinked. "You're not my sister?" she echoed. "Funny, you could have fooled me. How come you look like her, talk like her, dress like her and happen to be in the middle of her bedroom, wearing her dressing gown?"

Susan shook her head. It had been a crazy impulse to blurt out the truth. Not only would Mary Abbott not believe her, but she'd think she was crazy, as well.

She turned her face away from the little girl who would someday know her far too well. "Sorry, just a stupid joke on my part," she said in a deliberately casual voice. "Tell Mom I'll be down as soon as I change."

Mary didn't say a word, but Susan could feel her calm blue eyes surveying her. "You don't call her Mom," she said finally. "You call her Mummy, or Mother if you're annoyed with her, or sometimes even Elda. But you don't call her Mom."

Susan kept her back turned. "My mistake," she said. "Go away and let me get changed."

"You've never been particularly modest, either," Mary continued. "Unless you've got some new bruises you don't want me to see."

That startled Susan into turning around. "New bruises?"

"Check your arm. The old ones are probably faded by now, but there may be new ones."

Susan slid off the chenille bathrobe and surveyed her right arm. It was smooth and soft, without the firm muscle tone she was used to.

"The other arm," Mary said patiently.

They were fading now, a yellowish-purple memory on her upper arm. She stared down at the bruises in surprise. It would have taken a fair amount of force to leave that kind of mark on her.

"How did it happen?" she asked.

"You told me you walked into a door."

"But how could a door do that?"

"Exactly," Mary said. "So why don't you remember? I don't think you even know who I am."

"Of course I do. You're Mary Abbott, you're nine years old, born April 25, 1940, and you're my... sister." She barely hesitated.

Mary, with her precocious face, looked far from convinced. "He hit you, didn't he? Is he the reason you don't remember anything?"

"He didn't touch me!" Susan protested hotly.

"He was just sitting by the window, smoking, when I woke up and—"

"I'm not talking about Jack. Jack would never hit a woman, though he might be tempted. I'm talking about Neddie. He's the one who left those bruises on your arm, and it's not the first time he's done it. I can understand your lying to Daddy, but you don't need to keep it from me."

"Why would I lie to Daddy?"

"Because this marriage is too important for the family, and you know it. Daddy made a lot of money during the war, but it was all with Neddie's help. And things haven't been so good lately—I've heard Mummy and Daddy fighting about it. If you marry Neddie the business partnership goes through, and they'll build all those little boxy houses in all the poorer towns of Connecticut, New York and New Jersey. And the Abbotts will be very rich once more, and everyone will live happily ever after. Except poor Lou, who should have run when she had the chance."

Susan pulled the maroon dress over her head, searching and finally finding the zipper on the side of the dress, under her arm. She zipped it, then sat back down at the cluttered dressing table and stared in the mirror. Mary Abbott was reflected behind her, young and old at the same time, mother and sister, child and parent.

She turned to face her. "Do you trust me, Mary?"

"Yes."

"Then will you help me?"

"Help you get away from Neddie? Absolutely."

Susan shook her head. "I don't know if that's what I'm supposed to do. If that's the lesson I need to learn. I'm here for a reason, and I haven't the faintest idea what that reason is."

"You're here because you were born here," Mary said flatly.

Susan shook her head. "No, I wasn't. I was born twenty years from now. I'm not Tallulah Abbott. I'm her niece, Susan, and somehow I've gotten trapped inside her body."

Mary didn't say a word. She just looked at her for a long, solemn moment, then shook her head. "You expect me to believe that?"

"No."

Mary came up to her and put her small hands on Susan's face, cupping it as she looked deeply into her eyes. It was the strangest sensation—Susan had felt that loving touch, that gentle gaze many times in her life, but this time the hands were a child's hands, the eyes that looked into hers were innocent.

They stared at each other for a long, silent moment, and then Mary spoke. "If you're Lou's niece that would make you my daughter."

Knowing how absurd it would sound, Susan shut her eyes for a moment. "Yes."

Mary released her face, taking a brisk step backward. "I almost believe you."

"I know it's impossible to imagine, but...what?"

"I almost believe you," Mary said again. "Your eyes are different. They're the same shape, the same color, but there's someone else looking out of them. I'm guessing this is probably a dream, but I'll go along with it for now. What do you need from me?"

"Thank God," Susan breathed. "I need you to help cover for me. I only know the barest details of Tallulah's life and family. My mother...er, you... never talked much about her, or the family."

"You never met Tallulah? Why?"

Susan didn't want to tell her the truth. That Tallulah Abbott died on her wedding day, fifty years ago, three days from now. "She died young," she said evasively.

"How young?"

"I don't think you really want to know the future, do you? Besides, this is a dream. Personally I think it's my dream, not yours, but that doesn't matter. Sooner or later we'll both wake up and be back where we belong, and you don't need unhappy memories—"

"You die," Mary said flatly.

"No."

"All right, Tallulah dies," she corrected herself impatiently. "When?"

"I don't think—"

"If you want my help you'll have to tell me, or I'll go back downstairs and leave you to fend for yourself," Mary said in her mature little voice.

Susan took a deep breath. Mary had always been

a stubborn soul, and she had no doubt she meant what she said. "Three days from now," she said finally. "On her wedding day."

Mary took a deep, shuddering breath. "No," she protested.

Susan reached out a hand to touch her. "Well, I think it would be clear why I'm here. I'm supposed to stop it. Stop Tallulah from dying."

"You're right. You shouldn't be marrying Neddie, anyway, and we both know it. You'll have to call it off. If Lou doesn't get married, then the future will have to change."

"Maybe. It's the best I can come up with on short notice."

"You'd better come down to dinner," Mary said. "The sooner you face them all the easier it will be. You can say you've got a headache. You haven't been very talkative in the past few weeks, anyway, so no one will probably notice if you just sit there."

"And then what?"

"And then maybe we'll both wake up. And Lou will be back and everything will be all right."

"You're only nine, but I bet you know that doesn't happen," Susan said.

"Lou isn't going to die," Mary said fiercely.

"That's a promise," Susan said.

THE SHOES WERE HORRIBLE. High-stacked heels, when Susan hadn't worn anything but flats and running shoes for the past ten years. Her ankles almost collapsed as she made her way down the wide, winding staircase of the old Abbott mansion, but Mary was beside her, providing physical and moral support.

She'd seen photographs of the old house, and her mother had occasionally told her stories of it, but it still was far from what she imagined. She'd pictured something out of an old Cary Grant movie, but this place was in color, slightly shabby, as if there hadn't been enough money for new slipcovers or carpets in the past few years. The war hadn't been over for that long, Susan reminded herself. Maybe there was still a shortage of goods, even for wealthy people like the Abbotts of Connecticut.

The elderly man standing at the makeshift bar glared at her as she entered the room. "It's about time," he said. "You're too late for cocktails, but then, your mother's made up for it. The others are out on the patio—we'll go in for dinner now."

She stared at the querulous old man. He had to be her grandfather, Mary and Tallulah's father, the esteemed Ridley Abbott. He looked like an old man, and yet he couldn't be much older than fifty.

"Why don't I see if I can help serve?" she suggested.

"Don't be ridiculous. We have servants to take care of such things. Go find your mother and your fiancé and tell them you've finally decided to grace us with your presence." He whirled on Mary. "What are you staring at?"

"Nothing," Mary said in her admirably calm voice. "Lou and I will go call the others."

The old man's eyes narrowed in sudden suspicion. "Lou can get them by herself. I want to have a little talk with you."

Susan squashed down her sudden feeling of panic. She had absolutely no idea where the patio was, and if there was anyone out there besides Elda and Neddie she was going to be up a creek without a paddle.

"Not now, Daddy," Mary said. "You can yell at me after dinner. I'm too hungry right now."

"And whose fault is that? Your sister's, that's who. And now we've got that nosey parker here as well, which doesn't improve my disposition, let me tell you."

"Which nosey parker?"

"You know who I mean," Ridley said, pouring himself another glass of whisky. Straight. "I can't wait till this damned wedding is over."

"Neither can I," Susan murmured. But the old man had already dismissed her, concentrating on the dark amber of his drink.

She had no memory of her grandmother Elda—she'd left her husband sometime in the fifties and died a decade later, but Susan had always pictured a frail, white-haired old lady. The woman laughing with Neddie Marsden was a far cry from that image, with thick dark hair and a cocktail dress that was surprisingly daring for a mature woman. She threw a glance toward her elder daughter, and Susan was shocked to see the veiled dislike in her blue eyes.

"There's the little sleepyhead," she cooed in a deceptively cheery voice. "We were afraid you were going to sleep straight through dinner. Look who's decided to join us."

Neddie Marsden had changed very little in almost fifty years. She would have known him anywhere—the heavy-lidded eyes, the wide, thick-lipped mouth, the faint air of menacing charm. He was a hearty man, bluff and friendly, and he'd always been more than kind to Mary Abbott and her daughter. But looking at the younger version of Ned Marsden, she couldn't help but notice his solid, be-ringed fingers, and remember the fading bruises on Tallulah's upper arm.

"Hi, Ned," she said in her husky voice, making no effort to move closer.

"Is that any way to greet your fiancé?" Neddie chided her. He reached out and put that heavy hand on her arm, and Susan flinched, instinctively. Enough of Tallulah remained inside her to be wary.

She averted her face in time for Ned's wet mouth to land on her cheek, and if the fingers on her arm tightened slightly she couldn't be certain. "How nice to see you."

"Don't be ridiculous, Tallulah," her mother snapped. "You know Neddie comes for supper every night. But you haven't noticed who else is here. Say hello to your old friend Jack.'' There was no missing the trace of malice in Elda's arch voice.

Susan controlled the sinking feeling that hit her as she realized there was a third person on the flagstone patio. "Hello, Jack," she murmured.

"Long time, no see," Jack replied. "I came by to drop off a wedding present, and Elda was kind enough to invite me for dinner."

"How…lovely," Susan said in a faint voice. In the fading sunlight of an early-June evening Jack McGowan looked even more overwhelming. Compared to Jake Wyczynski's mode of dress McGowan looked positively formal, with his suit and white shirt and loosened tie. But compared to Ned and Ridley's pristine neatness it was clear that Jack McGowan was a vagabond.

"Do you want me to go tell Hattie we're ready to eat?" Mary piped up.

"Not quite, dear," Elda replied. "Why don't we go inside and let Tallulah and Jack have some time together to renew their acquaintance."

"I don't think so," Neddie rumbled, but Elda sidled up to him, frankly flirtatious, and put her hand on his arm.

"Now, Neddie, you're going to have to learn to listen to your mother-in-law's wishes. You don't have to be so possessive—Tallulah knows what's best for her. And you've seen how docile she's become in the past year. Why, you'd hardly recognize the flighty, passionate creature she used to be. Thank heavens.''

''Thank heavens,'' Neddie echoed, clearly unconvinced. ''I don't see why—''

''I need you to make me another drink, Neddie darling,'' Elda cooed. ''Ridley always makes mine too weak, and I'm afraid I have a naughty little habit of making mine too strong. Come along.''

Susan waited, holding her breath. Young Ned Marsden didn't seem like the kind of man who'd do anybody's bidding, much less that of his slightly inebriated future mother-in-law, but she'd underestimated Elda's charm. After a moment Neddie shrugged his massive shoulders and managed a tight smile.

''Behave yourself, Lou,'' he said in what was obviously supposed to be a playful tone of voice, chucking her under the chin. For some reason it sounded vaguely threatening.

Elda waited until Neddie preceded her into the house, then turned back. ''Come along, Mary.''

''I thought I'd keep them company—''

''I said come along. I'm sure Tallulah doesn't need you around helping her out.''

That's exactly what I need, Susan thought desperately. ''I don't mind, Mummy,'' she said.

Elda's smile was frosty. ''I do.''

Susan waited until the French doors closed behind them, wishing desperately for a drink or a cigarette. It didn't matter that she'd never smoked in her life—

her hands and her mouth needed one. And she hated hard liquor, blaming alcohol for her fatherless existence, but for some reason the cocktail in Jack's big, strong hand looked completely alluring.

"What was that all about?" she asked, resisting the impulse to ask him for a cigarette. She moved past him on her slightly wobbly high heels and sank down on one of those cast-iron lawn chairs.

"I think Elda's not quite sure whether she wants you to marry good old Neddie," Jack said in a level voice.

"Why not?"

"It looks like she fancies him herself. Of course, just because he's marrying you doesn't mean he'll stop fooling around. He doesn't strike me as the faithful-husband type. I wouldn't be surprised if he and Elda don't have a little something going on already."

"Don't be disgusting."

"Am I? I thought I was simply being frank. You could hardly consider this marriage to be the love match of the century. Especially considering Jimmy."

Susan's stomach knotted instinctively. "What about Jimmy?" she said. Where the hell was Mary when she needed her?

He took a deep, steadying breath. She'd thought he had short hair, but compared to the others he was practically shaggy. He ran a hand through his thick, rumpled hair, obviously looking for patience.

"Look, Lou, we might as well talk about it."

"Talk about what? Are you going to tell me I shouldn't marry Neddie?"

"He's a war profiteer. He made a fortune sitting on his butt at home while boys were dying overseas."

"Not very commendable, but I'm sure a great many people made money from the war. That's the problem with war—it can be very good for the economy."

"I'm not talking about a normal profit, Lou. I'm not talking about a decent profit. I'm talking about raking in a fortune selling shoddy goods and cheap parts to the government. Faulty parts that cost lives, just because of his greed."

"Have you got proof?" she demanded.

"I'm working on it."

"Why? Is it something to do with me?"

"Dream on, princess. You're not that important in the scheme of things. I'm a reporter, remember. It's my job to investigate things. I'm like a dog with a dead rat—I'm not letting go until I'm sure it's dead."

"Charming," Susan said faintly. "What do you intend to do?"

"Expose Neddie Marsden for the murderous bastard he is. And no, I'm not going to apologize for my language," he added. "I just thought I'd warn you. Your father was in that mess pretty deep as well, and I don't know if I can protect you. I certainly can't if you're going to go ahead and marry Marsden.''

"Why would you want to protect me? I thought I wasn't that important?''

"You aren't. But I'm fond of your little sister. And God knows Jimmy loved you. Maybe it's for his sake I'm giving you a chance.''

"Jimmy,'' she echoed in a pensive voice.

He came and sat down next to her, stretching his long legs out in front of him. He was taller than Ned Marsden, leaner, with a hint of coiled strength about him that was totally unlike Neddie's brute handsomeness. Oddly enough, there was nothing threatening about Jack's size, or strength. "We need to talk about it, Lou,'' he said gently.

"Talk about what?''

He shook his head. "It happened, Lou. Whether we like it or not, it happened, and pretending it didn't won't fix things.''

Oh, God, what had Tallulah done? It must have been pretty shocking. Had she slept with Jack McGowan?

She stalled for time. "If you want to talk about it go right ahead. I have nothing to say.'' Which was nothing more than the simple truth.

Jack sighed. "Look, we kissed. It was no big deal, it meant absolutely nothing and we both know it. We were both upset, talking about Jimmy, and it just happened. We don't need to feel like we've betrayed him. It was nothing.''

She had the strangest sensation, prickling at the back of her neck. "Where did you kiss me?" she demanded suddenly, not caring how odd it sounded.

"On the mouth, sweetheart."

She shook her head. "I mean, where in the house. Er...did anyone see us?"

"In the garage. And there was no one around. Your secret is safe."

In the garage. She'd known it. Susan turned to look at him, shielding her expression. At least Tallulah hadn't slept with him. But the truth was almost as bad. Because enough of Lou remained in that foreign body that Susan was now trapped in.

Kissing Jack McGowan wasn't "nothing." It was the most powerful experience in Tallulah Abbott's life, powerful enough that it crossed time and space and invaded Susan's soul.

"You're right," she said. "It didn't mean a thing."

"So then why have you been running away from me ever since?"

"I have nothing to say to you. I'm getting married, ready to start life as a wife and a mother. Jimmy's in the past. Jimmy's brother is in the past. I'm sorry if that sounds harsh, but it's simply the truth." The husky voice sounded calm and believable, but Jack didn't seem convinced.

"You love Neddie?"

"Yes."

"And you've forgotten about Jimmy?"

Dangerous ground, when in truth, Susan knew nothing at all about Jimmy McGowan. She relaxed and let her instincts, which seemed to belong to Tallulah, speak for her. "I loved Jimmy," she said. "But he's gone, and nothing will change that. I've let go of him. You need to let go of him, as well."

She expected that would drive him away, but he simply nodded. "You're right," he said. "I'm just not sure if I want to let go of you."

Chapter Eight

Susan was never quite sure how she made it through that horrendous dinner. It helped that she and Mary were roundly ignored by the others. Elda Abbott had had just enough to drink to make her the glittering center of attention. She flirted outrageously with all three of the men, ignored her two daughters, laughed too loudly, talked too much and spilled cigarette ashes all over her untouched dinner.

Ridley Abbott spent the dinner in silence, glaring at all and sundry. His few attempts at conversation were terse orders to Susan to look happier, but since Elda snapped at him the orders went unnoticed.

Neddie was a busy man. He consumed huge amounts of the bland food, smoked between courses, drank steadily, parried Elda's heavy-handed flirtation and cast constant, suspicious looks between Jack and Susan. Or Jack and Tallulah, Susan reminded herself. It was Tallulah they were all concerned with. Tallulah, who'd kissed her true love's brother in the ga-

rage, who was about to marry a bullying businessman with dubious ethics.

Jack didn't say a thing. Hadn't, since that surprising remark out on the patio. Susan had never even
heard of a Jack McGowan in her family's life—whatever role he'd played, it had obviously been a minor
one.

By the time the cook had begun to serve dessert,
the air was blue with smoke, and Susan was feeling
faintly nauseous. "I think I'll go to bed," she murmured. "I'm not feeling well."

"It's early!" Neddie protested. "We need to
talk."

"Now, Neddie, can't you see Tallulah needs her
beauty sleep?" Elda said playfully. "You'll have the
rest of your lives to talk. You go ahead, darling, and
take Mary with you. I'll entertain the men."

I'm sure you will, Susan thought, managing a tight
smile. She pushed back her chair, and all the men
rose, perfectly polite in their latent hostility.

"Come on, kid," she muttered to Mary. "We
know when we're not wanted."

Her room was chilly, but then, for the first time in
her life Susan was having trouble getting warm. She
sank down on the bed as Mary shut the door behind
them.

"That bitch," Susan muttered.

Mary looked completely horrified. "Women don't
curse!"

"I do. That woman downstairs is a bitch and a

half, and I don't care if she is yours and Tallulah's mother," Susan said frankly, kicking off the dreaded high heels.

"She's not. Our mother, that is. You're right about the rest of it, though. She is a—" Words failed her.

"Say *bitch*, Mary," Susan ordered. "You're old enough to use the right word when it's called for."

"She's not very nice," Mary said reprovingly, reminding Susan of the woman she'd become. Fifty-nine-year-old Mary Abbott never spoke ill of anyone if she could help it. "Our mother died before the war, and Elda moved in on Daddy when he was most vulnerable."

"Then why do we call her 'Mummy'?"

"Because she hates it," Mary said with a grin.

"Good girl," Susan murmured. "And who are the McGowans? I gather Jimmy's dead, but who is Jack and what does he want with Tallulah?"

"You grew up with them. Well, with Jimmy really—Jack was older. You and Jimmy were best friends growing up, and you always said you were going to get married. But you always had a huge crush on Jack, even when you were fighting with him."

"And what did Jack feel about Lou?"

Mary shrugged. "You were his brother's girl-friend. I don't think he thought much beyond that. He was going out with real women, and you were just a kid with a crush on him. I'm not sure he even knew."

"Did Jimmy know?"

"Jimmy knew Lou better than she knew herself. I don't think he minded. He always worshiped his older brother. Don't you remember…no, of course you don't."

"Remember what?"

"Lou showed me a letter Jimmy sent her. It arrived after he was killed, and it was kinda nice but kinda creepy. It was like he knew he was going to die. And he said that if something happened to him you should marry Jack. That Jack would take care of you."

"I don't need anyone to take care of me," Susan shot back.

"Lou doesn't, either. But you know men—they don't realize that. They think women are fragile little flowers who have to be protected from life."

"Poor Lou," Susan murmured. "And what does Jack think about all this? Does he know his brother thought he should take on his fiancée?"

"I don't think so. It wouldn't matter—I can't see Jack doing anything he doesn't want to do, even for Jimmy's sake, and he really loved Jimmy."

Susan leaned back on the bed, reaching up to touch her mouth. He'd kissed her. Kissed Tallulah, that was. In the garage, just as Jake Wyczynski had kissed Susan. And she wondered what it had been like. Whether it was as unsettling as Jake's kiss had been to a much more experienced Susan Abbott.

She felt so strange, like she was floating somewhere in space, looking down at Tallulah Abbott fifty years in the past. She touched her face, and it felt like her face and yet it wasn't. Her body, and yet Tallulah's.

"You need to sleep," Mary announced in a gently critical voice. "With any luck this is all some crazy dream. You'll wake up tomorrow and be Lou again."

"I'd rather wake up and be Susan." She shivered, still unaccountably cold. "Back in my own time."

"Maybe you will," Mary said. She pulled a blanket around Susan, tucking it against her with gentle hands, and Susan looked up at her in surprise. It was so very strange, to see this little girl taking care of her with instinctive maternal care.

"If I'm gone I want you to know something," Susan said suddenly. "You're a wonderful mother. The best anyone could hope for."

Mary grinned, suddenly looking no more than her nine years of age. "That's encouraging to hear. And what about your father? Is he wonderful, too?"

Susan bit her lip. "I don't think I should tell you too much about the future. You're probably better off not knowing."

"That doesn't sound very cheerful. I want to be a world-famous diplomat, I want to marry William Holden, and I want to win an Oscar and have five children. Are you going to tell me that won't happen?" There was humor in her young voice.

"Those are pretty grandiose dreams."

"That's what being young is all about. At least I

know I can manage the five children," Mary said. "The rest will happen if I work hard enough for it."

"Anything can happen if you work hard enough and dream hard enough," Susan said. "You taught me that."

Mary shook her head. "Go to sleep, Lou. I enjoyed meeting my daughter, even if I think you're a little bit screwy."

"I enjoyed meeting you, Mary."

The room was still and dark when Mary closed the door behind her. Susan nestled down on the bed, shivering slightly in the warm night air. She ought to get up and take off these horrendously uncomfortable clothes. In particular, the bra and girdle that seemed like medieval instruments of torture. She definitely wasn't made for time travel. At least she hadn't gone back to the time of whalebone corsets. Rubber was bad enough.

She closed her eyes and let the night fold quietly around her. This had to be a strange, twisted sort of dream. Did people go to sleep in dreams? Did they dream within dreams? She had no idea. All she knew was that she wanted to wake up in her own bed, in her own decade. She didn't want to be here, trapped in Lou's body. She didn't want to marry the wrong man.

And she didn't want to die in less than three days.

JACK MCGOWAN LIT a cigarette as he strolled toward his venerable Studebaker. It was an old car, prewar, and ran like a top. His mother wanted him to buy a newer one, something with a little more style, but he was resisting. Just as he was resisting all the plans they'd made for him.

Hell, he wasn't the only man who was having a hard time settling down after a war that had been over for four years. And he hadn't even served—they'd told him he was too valuable as a war correspondent to waste his time in uniform.

But now the war was over. The battles had faded, and he was stuck back in the states, covering society weddings.

He needed to get the hell out of there. And in truth, he'd asked for this assignment. This wasn't a café society wedding, this was a merger between a shady businessman and one of his patsies.

And Lou Abbott was stuck in the middle, the perfect pawn.

She'd changed so damned much he couldn't believe it. He'd known her all his life—at one point his parents and the Abbotts had been friends. She'd always been around—a scrawny, long-legged kid with braids hanging halfway down her skinny arms, a tomboy with her heart in her eyes. He'd called her Spider when she was twelve and taller than Jimmy.

She and Jimmy had been inseparable, best buddies from the moment they first met. There were times when he'd almost been jealous of that. Particularly when he'd come home toward the end of the war and found she'd grown up.

She'd been seventeen then, and her coltish look had filled out into a prematurely voluptuous beauty. She'd still had that wild, boyish, mischievous streak, but it had matured along with her lush body.

And so had the powerful crush he'd always known she harbored for him. But she wasn't watching him anymore, she only had eyes for Jimmy.

If she'd been a year older they would have married before Jimmy shipped out. If Jimmy had been a year younger the war would have been over before he was sent overseas, and he'd be alive today, the kid brother who'd always been some kind of anchor for Jack.

Lots of "ifs." But Jimmy had died, and something had happened to Lou. Some light had been turned down, so low it was barely burning. If she married a lying bully like Neddie Marsden that light would go out forever.

The last time he'd seen her had been a little more than a year ago. Jimmy had been dead for two years, and he'd been avoiding coming home, avoiding the terrible truth that if he came back without Jimmy he'd know that Jimmy wasn't coming back. But his mother had gotten sick, and he hadn't been able to put it off any longer, and he'd come back...and gone to see Lou.

She'd been in the garage behind the house, alone. Mary was in school, Elda was a clubwoman, and only Hattie was there in the kitchen, looking at him out of her warm brown eyes as she sent him to find Lou.

Lou had always been surprisingly good at machinery, and she was bent over the engine of her blue roadster, frowning with concentration, and he stopped and watched her covertly for a moment. Thinking about what Jimmy had lost.

Thinking about what he'd thrown away.

And then she saw him, and her face lit up with a smile, and she dropped the wrench she was holding and ran toward him like the tomboy she'd once been.

And then she stopped short of flinging herself in his arms, remembering. Remembering too much.

"Hi, Jack," she said. He'd dreamed about her husky voice—long, erotic dreams that made him feel as if he was betraying his kid brother.

"Hey, Lou," he said. "I wanted to come by and see how you were doing."

"I'm fine. College is great, I've got a new car, and—" Her bright voice faded, her face crumpled, and she threw herself into his arms.

It hurt more than he could have imagined. For three years he'd held his emotions in check, and now Lou's sobbing brought it all back. He missed his brother, damn it. He missed him like hell.

He didn't know how he managed to end up kissing her. It just happened. The feel of her warm, soft body against his, the swell of her breasts, the scent of perfume and flowers and the hot sun. And Jimmy was dead, and Lou was alive, in his arms, and he just kissed her.

And she kissed him back. It was no sisterly kiss, no closemouthed, Hollywood kiss simulating passion. He tipped her head back and kissed her hard, and she answered him with awkward, desperate passion. As if she knew their chances were running out and she was scared.

He didn't know what had broken their embrace. Maybe it was the distant slam of a car door, maybe it was the wind, maybe it was his guilty conscience for trying to steal his kid brother's girl. All he knew was that she'd shoved him away, a look of such grief and horror on her face that his desire had vanished.

And that was the last time he'd seen her until tonight, when he'd conned his way past Hattie and gone to her bedroom, planning to leave a note for her, only to find her sleeping like a baby in her rumpled wedding gown.

He should have left. He should never have gone to her bedroom in the first place, and once he saw she was there he should have slunk away like a junkyard dog.

But she'd looked like Sleeping Beauty, and he'd wanted to kiss her awake. She looked like every dream he'd ever had, everything he'd wanted and given up on long ago. And instead he'd taken a seat by the window and watched her as she slept.

She was a fool to marry a heel like Neddie Marsden. For three years Jack had been trying to prove that Marsden's company had siphoned off illegal profits from the war effort, and gotten rich by doing it. Gotten rich from the blood of America's fighting men. And old man Abbott, who'd never liked the upstart McGowan boys, had gotten rich, as well.

Now he was trading his older daughter...for what? For more money? For protection? And Lou, with the life almost gone from her huge, beautiful brown eyes, looked as if she'd given up fighting.

Damn, he wished Jimmy were still here. Jimmy would never have let something like this happen. If Jimmy hadn't been killed in France during the last days of the war, he'd be back home, married to Lou, and there would already be at least one baby on the way.

And just maybe Jack wouldn't have minded.

But he minded like hell a war profiteer like Marsden ending up with Jimmy's true love. And he wasn't about to let that happen.

He had two days to stop it. So far he'd been unable to get enough proof that Marsden was crooked, and he was ready to give up trying. He had to get on with his life. He couldn't bring Neddie down without toppling the mighty Abbotts, as well, and while he didn't give a tinker's damn about Elda and Ridley, Lou and her little sister were a different matter. He didn't want to see their lives ruined.

But he could keep Lou from wrecking her future by marrying the wrong man.

Tomorrow they were holding a rehearsal dinner,

and all it had taken was a little well-applied flirtation, and Elda had invited him, despite Neddie's glower. He'd find time to talk to Lou once more, to try to convince her that she was making the mistake of her life. It was up to her whether she'd listen or not.

At least he would know he had done his damnedest, for Jimmy's sake and for Lou's. He was going back overseas—he had an offer to work for one of the foreign news bureaus, and he found he'd developed a bad case of itchy feet. America didn't seem like home anymore. There were too many places to see, too much stuff going on in a world turned upside down by the cataclysmic war.

Most people he knew were buying those tiny little houses Levitt and Marsden and others were putting up. They were settling down to a safe, carefully circumscribed life.

It wasn't for him.

Funny, but he wouldn't have thought it was for the likes of Lou Abbott, either. As a kid she'd always been full of imagination and adventure, longing for distant lands and travel. Life must have beaten that out of her.

But he still wasn't going to stand by and let her tie herself to Neddie Marsden without her knowing exactly what she was getting into. Maybe Jack couldn't pin anything on him, but sooner or later someone would, and Lou would be dragged down with him. If he gave her a chance to escape he would have done his duty.

And then he could leave for Asia with a clear conscience, and just maybe, when he ran into her again, he'd finally be over her.

And maybe pigs would fly.

MARY ABBOTT PUSHED her silvery hair back with a weary hand, closing the bedroom door as she stepped back. "She must be exhausted, poor girl," she murmured.

Alex Donovan stood watching her, his expression giving nothing away. "She's not sick, is she?"

"Just worn-out. You don't realize how much work a formal wedding is."

"No, I suppose I don't. Do you suppose we would have had better luck if we'd had one?"

Mary shook her head, a regretful smile on her face. "They never would have let us get that far. That's why we eloped, remember?"

"I remember," he said. "Are they why you left?"

"Don't," Mary said. She leaned her head against the closed door for a moment, taking a deep, calming breath. "I don't need to worry about her, do I?" she asked, knowing she sounded helpless, somehow not minding. In Susan's thirty years she'd never been able to turn to Susan's father for support.

"Not about Susan," he said. "You raised her well, Mary. She's a fighter. I think you're right—her body's worn-out and needs to recoup its strength. She'll wake up when she's ready to."

"She's slept all day."

"She'll be all right, Mary," he said, putting his hands on her shoulders. The touch, after so many years, was still familiar. "Trust me," he said.

"Yes," she said. And she knew, deep in her heart, that she always had.

Chapter Nine

The sun was beating against her closed eyes, but Susan was afraid to move. She wanted to postpone the moment as long as she could, the realization that her dream wasn't over yet. The bed was soft beneath her, the faint smell of old cigarettes clung to the pillow and sheets, and she was still back in 1949, about to marry the wrong man, about to die within hours of making that mistake.

There used to be some television show about someone who traveled through time, trying to fix people's mistakes. She'd never been into TV much, except for old movies, but she'd seen an episode or two and liked it. Maybe that was why she was here. To stop her aunt Tallulah from making the mistake of her life. To change history. And then Tallulah might still be alive.

Except this wasn't an episode of "Quantum Leap," and there was no gorgeous actor around. Well, Jack McGowan did happen to be unsettlingly attractive, but he wasn't the one traveling through time. And neither was she. This was a dream, a crazy, mixed-up dream, brought on by the stress of the wedding. She simply needed to get through it and she'd wake up back in her own bed, ready for her own wedding.

She grabbed the chenille bathrobe and headed for the luxurious pink-tiled bathroom, which Mary had assured her was the recently remodeled height of modern plumbing conveniences. There was no shower stall, but the huge tub at least came equipped with a shower head, and even smoked-glass doors, and she had every intention of getting thoroughly clean. She couldn't wait to get the smell of cigarettes out of her hair.

She hadn't taken into account how strange it would be to brush someone else's teeth. Her mouth wasn't that dissimilar from what Susan was used to, but the body was strange indeed. She'd never soaped such ample breasts before, and the flesh beneath her hands was softer, less muscled than the body she was used to. Obviously women in the late nineteen forties didn't work out.

There was no way in hell she was going to put on that horrific girdle again, though she had no choice with the holsterlike bra that turned Lou's already generous endowments into Madonnalike missiles. It took her forever to find a pair of baggy Levi's, and she almost wept with relief when she did. There were no T-shirts, of course, but she found an oversize man's dress shirt that worked perfectly if she tied the tails in front of her. She even found a pair of blue sneakers, and for the first time she began to feel slightly human, even with the unfamiliar mane of long wet hair trailing down her back.

There was no sign of anyone else as she made her way down to the kitchen, in desperate need of coffee. The comfortable-looking woman who worked as the Abbotts' maid stood at the stove, busy with something, but she looked up when Susan walked in. Hattie, her name was, Susan remembered. She was someone her mother still occasionally talked about. Hattie had been more of a mother to Mary Abbott than anyone.

"'Morning, Miss Lou," she greeted her placidly. "You're up early this morning. You don't usually get out of bed before nine."

Susan glanced at the clock on the wall. It was seven-thirty in the morning—no wonder the house was quiet.

"I was too restless," she said, sliding into one of the kitchen chairs and yawning. "I couldn't sleep any longer. Maybe I'll go for a run."

"A run? Now why on earth would you want to do a fool thing like that?"

Oops, Susan thought. "Well, a brisk walk. I need some fresh air. Something to clear my head."

"You didn't have anything to drink last night, sugar. Why would you need to clear your head? Unless you're thinking twice about marrying that young man of yours." Her voice was soft and noncommittal, but Susan didn't miss the faint undertone.

"You don't like Neddie, do you?"

Hattie turned to look at her. "Mr. Marsden's all right," she said carefully. "If he's what you want, then that's fine. I just hope you know what you're doing, Miss Lou. I've taken care of you since you were a little baby, and you're like one of my own. I don't want to see you getting hurt."

"I'll be okay, Hattie," she said. Wishing she could be sure of any such thing.

"You go on into the dining room, and I'll bring you your tea, baby," Hattie said.

"Er...I'd rather have coffee if that's okay. And couldn't I just have it here with you?"

Hattie stared at her. "Miss Lou, you never liked coffee. And your mama would have a fit if she found you in here eating with the help."

"She's not my mother, and I really don't care what she thinks," Susan said. "And I'm in a coffee kind of mood. If you don't mind the company?"

Hattie gave her a radiant smile. "I'm gonna miss you, Miss Lou. If it weren't for Miss Mary, I'd finish up here. Things have never been the same since your real mama died." She set a cup and saucer down on the oilcloth-covered table in front of Susan, then poured her a cup of oily black stuff out of the aluminum percolator on the stove. "You gonna keep your promise to your little sister?"

"Don't I always keep my promises?" Susan replied, hedging. The coffee was too strong and almost flavorless, but she suspected that was more a fault of the can of supermarket coffee sitting on the counter than Hattie's culinary failings. She dumped some sugar in it and drank it, anyway.

"This is no house for a little girl. Even if you can't take her to live with you like you promised, maybe you could arrange for her to visit. If Mr. Marsden doesn't mind. If he doesn't want her around, maybe you could arrange for her to go away to boarding school. I think Miss Mary would like that."

"He'll want her around," Susan said firmly, remembering the fading bruises on her arm, and wondering if bringing Mary into that household would be taking her from the frying pan into the fire.

For that matter, what was Tallulah thinking of, marrying a man who hurt her? If he had no qualms about bruising her before marriage, what would stop him once she was his legal property? And Susan had no doubt Neddie Marsden would consider any wife of his just that. His possession.

No, she had to stop the wedding. If this was some kind of weird, time-travel experience then it was her chance to change history and save Tallulah's life. If it really was a dream, then there'd be no harm done.

But how would Neddie Marsden take to being jilted the day before his wedding?

"Everything's going to be fine, Hattie," she said calmly. "I promise you."

"I surely do hope you're right, Miss Lou," Hattie

murmured, looking doubtful. She glanced out the kitchen window to the formal gardens, her broad face creasing. "Now what is that man doing here at this hour?" she said, but there was affection in her voice. "It's too early for visiting."

A sudden chill went through Susan's body. Or was it Lou's? "Neddie's here?" she demanded, unable to hide her alarm.

"No, ma'am. It's that Jack McGowan." Hattie tried to sound disapproving and failed completely. It was clear she had a fondness for the man. "You take him a cup of coffee and get rid of him, you hear? If Mr. Marsden was to show up there might be trouble."

"Why would Neddie show up?"

Hattie shrugged her solid shoulders beneath the starched uniform. "He likes to keep tabs on you. You know that. Now see what Mr. Jack wants and then get rid of him before there's trouble."

At that moment Susan thought she'd rather face a grizzly bear, or at least Tallulah's unpleasant fiancé, than deal with Jack McGowan first thing in the morning. Whoever and whatever she was, she was far too vulnerable to him, and it only complicated an already-difficult situation.

She stepped out onto the flagstone patio in the early-morning sunshine, the coffee in her hand. "Hey," she said.

"Hey, yourself," he replied, looking up at her. Reaching a hand up to shade the glare of the rising sun behind her, as if he couldn't quite believe what he was seeing.

"Hattie sent me out with a cup of coffee for you and strict orders to get rid of you," she said cheerfully, coming down the stone steps and into the shadows. "What do you want?"

"I promised Mary I'd help her with something," he murmured absently, taking the delicate cup from her hands. He should be drinking from a mug, she thought, but obviously people didn't use mugs in 1949, just those delicate, hardly hold anything teacups.

"What?"

He took a deep drink, obviously stalling. "Hattie makes some of the best coffee in the world," he said.

Susan kept a straight face at that one. "Are you going to keep acting like a television commercial or are you going to answer my question?"

"Television?" he echoed, startled. "I didn't know the lordly Abbotts owned such a plebian appliance."

"They don't," she said, guessing. "But the ads must be the same as the radio, right?"

"With the added benefit of pictures," he drawled. "What's between Mary and me is a secret. She likes surprises, and she doesn't realize what a joke this wedding is. I think she just wants to get the happy couple a wedding present."

"It's not a joke..."

"Okay, okay," he muttered, draining the coffee. "You want to tell me why you're dressed like that?"

She glanced down at the jeans, the white shirt, her sneakered feet. "It's comfortable. I'll have to dress up later so I might as well wear what I want now."

He reached out a hand and caught one long, damp strand of hair. It curled lightly against his fingers. "I've never seen you without your hair curled and arranged, your clothes just right. I sure as hell have never seen you without makeup."

"Sorry," she said, unrepentant. "Now you get to see what a hag I really am."

"Not quite," he murmured. "Why are you wearing my shirt?"

She glanced down, startled. "What makes you think this is yours?"

"Because I gave it to you, five years ago, after the dance at the country club. You had a fight with your parents and you'd taken off, and by the time I found you you'd fallen and skinned your elbow. Like the perfect gentleman I always am, I gave you the shirt off my back to bind your wounds and then drove you home."

"You drove me home shirtless? Doesn't sound gentlemanly to me," she said, trying to disguise her feverish thoughts. Why did Tallulah still hold on to Jack's shirt?

"I was wearing an undershirt, sweetheart. And trust me, you were too distraught to be seduced by my manly charms. I was only sorry Jimmy wasn't around to take care of you, but he'd already shipped out." He reached out and touched the shirt, just above her left breast, and for the first time she noticed the faint rust-colored stain of old blood. "That's how I know it's mine."

"Don't start imagining things, Jack," she said. "I only held on to it because it's comfortable. It's the only thing that goes with my jeans."

"Your jeans? Oh, you mean your dungarees."

Damn. "Jeans, dungarees, blue jeans, Levi's. Whatever you want to call them," she said carelessly. "I couldn't very well steal my father's old shirts—he's too short."

"Yeah," Jack said. "Mine fits you."

There was a sudden, strained silence between the two of them. The air smelled of a cool summer morning, and in the distance she could hear birds singing. His dark eyes slid over her, over the shirt she'd wrapped around her body, and it was like a caress, hot and intensely physical, and she wished to heaven that she'd opted for a girdle and seamed stockings.

"Don't marry him, Lou," he said quietly. "It would break Jimmy's heart."

"Jack…"

"Don't get me wrong, he'd want you to get married. Just not to Neddie Marsden. He's a crook, Lou. A cheap, lousy war profiteer, a bully and braggart and just the kind of man who'd break your heart."

"No, he isn't," she said.

"You think he's some kind of tin god? Because I always thought you were smarter than that."

"I'm not arguing with anything you say about

him,'' she said. "He's just not going to break my heart.''

"He'll cheat on you. Hell, he already has someone on the side.''

"Most likely,'' she said in that calm, husky voice she was growing eerily used to. "But it won't break my heart. That happened when Jimmy died, and nothing is ever going to hurt me like that again. It's impossible. Neddie will make a good enough husband. He wants me because I'm pretty and because I'm an Abbott. I suppose that sounds conceited but it's not. He doesn't care about who I am, what I think about, care about. He just wants me as a decoration.

"And that's fine with me. I need to get out of this house, and there's no way I can support myself. There aren't any jobs for women right now, and you know it. Too many GIs with families to support. So if I'm going to get out of here, and take Mary with me, I'm going to have to take my best offer, and that's Neddie. And frankly, I don't mind if he cheats on me. I'm hoping after the novelty of marriage wears off, he'll pretty much leave me in peace.''

Jack stared at her in consternation. "That's a hell of a future, Lou. Don't you think you deserve better?''

"A lot of people deserve better than they get. Jimmy didn't deserve to die. But life isn't fair.''

"Hell no, it isn't fair,'' he said. "But that doesn't mean *you* have to take a dive. I thought you were a fighter. I didn't think you'd let them beat you.''

It stung, his casual contempt. Somehow in the last,

uncharted time since she'd woken up in Tallulah Abbott's body, she'd become Lou. She might not have Lou's memory or familiarity with life in 1949, but she had Lou's emotions, Lou's longings and loyalties and slow, deep despair. She looked at Jack McGowan and knew she had Lou's passion, as well. For the wrong man.

"Sometimes you get tired of fighting," she said.

"Not the Lou Abbott I know. Not Jimmy's Lou."

"I'm not Jimmy's Lou any longer!" she shot back, feeling dangerously close to tears.

He shook his head. "No," he said. "You're not. You're a coward, taking the easy way out. Well, you don't have to worry about me. I'm not going to blow the whistle on Marsden. I don't have enough to pin anything on him, and I don't want to do something that might destroy you—your family." She might have missed the slight slip, but she didn't.

"Very noble," she said drily, mocking him, angry and miserable and guilty.

"Not particularly." Before she realized what he intended he'd taken a step toward her, sliding one hand beneath her tangle of wet hair to cup her neck. "Take care of yourself, kid," he murmured. "'Cause I won't be around to do it."

She was frozen, staring up at him. He'd nicked himself shaving that morning, and his brown eyes were flecked with gold. She looked at him and felt a deep surge of longing race through her, sharp and painful and completely overwhelming.

"I don't need looking after," she said. Making no effort to break away.

"Like hell," he muttered, and kissed her.

It was shockingly foreign and completely familiar, his hard, hot mouth against hers, pushing her lips open, tasting of coffee and toothpaste. She remembered his mouth, somewhere deep in some distant memory, and she remembered another mouth, another hot beat of longing that transcended common sense and even sanity.

She stopped thinking. She slid her arms around his waist, plastering her body against his, and she made a soft, moaning sound of surrender in the back of her throat. She'd been so cold, and now she was blazing hot, her body on fire, tasting his tongue in her mouth, feeling the strength of his hard body against hers, his hand closing over her breast, his leg nudging between her thighs.

She wouldn't have pushed him away, she would have let him lay her down on the flagstone terrace and take her there in full view of the bedroom windows, when Hattie's voice called out to her from the kitchen.

"Yoo-hoo, Miss Tallulah! Telephone for you."

Jack let go of her immediately, as if she were a hot potato, taking a step back as if to avoid further contamination. She forced herself to look at him. His breathing was ragged, his eyes almost black, his expression unreadable.

"Better go, Lou," he said in a rough voice. "It's probably your fiancé calling you. But remember one thing during your long, empty years. He'll never give you what you need.''

The words stung, almost as much as her mouth. ''And what are you offering, Jack?'' she mocked him. ''I haven't heard you come up with any alternatives.'' Say something, she thought. Ask me and I'll come with you.

But he said nothing.

She wanted to slap him. Something childish, out of an old movie, she wanted to give him such a crack across the face that the sound of it echoed through the town of Matchfield.

But she didn't. ''Have a nice life, Jack,'' she said carelessly. And she turned and ran up the stairs, back to the kitchen.

''My, my, Miss Lou!'' Hattie greeted her. ''Are you sure you ought to be doing that kind of thing the day before you're getting married?'' Oddly enough her brown eyes looked more sympathetic than condemning. ''You're just lucky your parents are sleeping in. What do you think would have happened if they woke up and happened to look out the window?''

''I don't know,'' she said listlessly.

''You're marrying the wrong man, child,'' Hattie said.

''I know,'' Susan said. Or was she Lou? She didn't know anymore. ''But the right man didn't ask me.''

Chapter Ten

Susan already knew what she faced on the second day of her life in the first half of the century. It was the day before the wedding, and the Abbotts didn't do things halfway. In about three hours everything would start, and she probably wouldn't have a moment to herself until—

Until when? Until she died? Is that what it would take to send her back to her own time? To stop this dream which was rapidly turning into a nightmare?

The rehearsal was set for noon at St. Anne's Episcopal Church, followed by a huge supper for wedding party members, relatives and anyone else they could drag in. And then tomorrow, at eleven o'clock in the morning, Tallulah Abbott would marry Edward Marsden. And she'd be dead before midnight.

How had Lou died? Was it in a train wreck? What had once been an unimportant detail now loomed very large indeed. If Lou Abbott died in a train, then Susan Abbott had every intention of driving a car wherever she went.

Hattie was watching her closely, her brown eyes suspicious. "What can I get you for breakfast, Miss Lou?"

"I'm not really hungry."

"Gotta keep your strength up. You got a busy day today. Let me make you some scrambled eggs and toast."

Susan shuddered. "Thanks, Hattie, but I don't think I could manage to choke it down. Maybe just some strawberry yogurt if we have some?"

"Yogurt? What's that?"

Good God, they didn't even have yogurt in 1949! There was no reasonable answer she could come up with. "How about cornflakes?" she guessed. Surely they had cornflakes back then.

"Miss Tallulah, you've always hated cereal. You know milk gives you gas. What is going on with you, child?"

"I don't know," Susan said truthfully. "I really don't know." Hattie was watching her with both doubt and wisdom in her eyes, and for a brief moment Susan was tempted to tell her the truth. Maybe Hattie would tell Lou's parents, and they'd lock her up in an insane asylum, but at least she wouldn't marry the wrong man. And at least she wouldn't die in a train wreck.

However, she might spend her days in a straitjacket, assuming they had such things, which wasn't much of an alternative. But then, Hattie didn't look like the type to rat on her.

"I need..." she began, when the doorbell rang.

"You just wait right here, Miss Lou. I'll get rid of whoever it is, and you can tell me all about it."

But Susan had already chickened out. "That's all right," she said brightly. "You're in the midst of something. I'll get the door." And she slipped out of the kitchen before she could change her mind.

The Abbott house was large and rambling, and she hadn't yet discovered where the front door was, so by the time she found it, whoever was waiting had stopped ringing the bell and had begun pounding on the door.

She yanked the door open, not surprised to be confronted by Neddie Marsden in a towering rage. "Stop making such a racket," she said calmly. "You'll wake the entire family."

He didn't move. He stood in the doorway, staring at her, his handsome face slack-jawed with shock, though she couldn't figure out why.

"What the hell do you think you're doing?" he demanded.

Susan had never responded particularly well to men having temper tantrums, and she wasn't going to let a petty tyrant like Neddie Marsden browbeat her. "Go away, Neddie," she said wearily. "I'm not in the mood for this so early in the morning...."

He caught her arm in a painful grip, pushing her into the house, and kicked the door shut behind him. He slammed her against the wall, pressing his bulk against her, and his fingers dug into the soft flesh of her upper arm. His nostrils were flaring and veins stood out in his temples.

"What's going on with you?" he demanded in a furious whisper. "What the hell do you think you're wearing? You look like a damned tomboy! You get your fanny upstairs and put on a dress, fix your hair and your makeup, and then you come back down and behave yourself."

She glared up at him, uncowed. "I'll dress any way I please. No one's coming over for hours, you weren't supposed to be here, and I have every right—"

He caught her other arm, as well, and shook her, hard enough that her head slammed against the wall behind her. "You have no rights. You're going to be my wife, and I expect you to behave like a lady at all times. I won't have you shaming me, Tallulah. I thought you were past all that wildness. I thought you'd grown up."

"What if I don't want to grow up?" She was proud of how even her tone of voice was. She didn't want to admit it, but pompous old Neddie Marsden was scaring her. Maybe because right now he wasn't old at all, he was young and strong and mean.

"You don't have the choice."

"What if I don't want to marry you?"

The expression on his face was absolutely terrifying. Her arms were numb beneath his punishing grip, and she couldn't move, she could only stand there, frozen.

"You're marrying me all right, Tallulah," he said in an icy voice. "You have no choice in the matter, I thought that was understood. I'd hate to have to threaten you..."

"You already are." She glared up at him, but her voice wavered.

"We've been through all this. Look on it as a simple business agreement. I get the wife and hostess I need, a blue-blooded Abbott to assure my place in society. In return, your father's estate is secure, and he doesn't have to worry about prosecution for war profiteering."

"You were the war profiteer, not my father," she shot back, remembering Jack's words.

"Hell, Tallulah, we both were. There's a lot of money to be made during wars, and we were smart enough to make it. Who do you think pays for those pretty dresses you hate wearing, for your new car, for this lavish wedding? Not even the Abbotts could survive the depression with their fortunes intact, though your father put up a good front. But he needed me. And in return, I get you."

"And what do I get out of the deal?" she demanded bitterly.

"I don't think anyone really cares," Neddie said softly. "You'll have an extravagant life-style and the respect due my wife, but those things never mattered to you, did they?"

"No," she said. "They never did."

"And then there's your little sister. You wouldn't

want to see her shamed, now would you? If your father was disgraced, her life would be ruined, and she wouldn't even have the cushion of money to help her. But we don't have to worry about that, now, do we? You're going to marry me, and you know it. No more disrespectful behavior, no more inappropriate clothing. And no more Jack McGowan.'' The fingers on her arms tightened still further, and she couldn't control her little cry of pain. ''I don't want him sniffing around you. I might have to do something about it, and you wouldn't want to get me angry, now would you, Tallulah?''

I'm not Tallulah, she wanted to cry, but she didn't. ''You're hurting me.''

''I don't care.''

''You'll leave bruises. Do you want the wedding guests to know that you hurt me? And that you enjoy it?''

He considered it for a moment, savoring the notion, and Susan's blood went cold. In a moment of blinding clarity she thought she knew how Tallulah had died, and it wasn't in a train wreck. It had been at the brutal hands of Edward Marsden.

He released her then, and she fell back against the wall, strangely weak. ''Go change, Tallulah,'' he said in his mellifluous voice. ''Fix your hair, put on some makeup. Take your time. I expect you to be a credit to me, and I'm prepared to wait.''

She stared at him. He was a big man, though not much taller than Tallulah's impressive height. He had cold, piggy eyes and a cruel smile, and she realized with a start that he wasn't that old. Probably not even thirty, and yet old in the harsh ways of the world.

She pushed away from the wall, and he stepped back, smugly sure he had her beaten. "You'll have a long wait," she said.

"I'm patient," he said. "And I always win."

She believed him. She remembered the ancient Ned Marsden with his cowed second wife and his milky eyes, still radiating power even in his late seventies. It wouldn't do to underestimate him.

She turned to leave him, and his voice followed her. "I'm counting on you, Tallulah. You wouldn't want to see me lose my temper."

He was right about that much. He could lose his temper all he wanted, once she was out of reach. She said nothing, feeling his cold eyes on her back as she mounted the stairs, only to have Lou's father almost barrel into her in his anxiety to get down.

"What have you done?" he demanded in a furious whisper. "You haven't made him angry, have you?"

She looked at the man who raised her mother. He was a frightened, selfish little man, ready to sacrifice his own daughter to keep himself safe.

She didn't bother to disguise the contempt in her face. "I'm sure you'll fix everything." She moved past him, her back straight.

His voice followed her. "For God's sake, change those awful clothes! You'll ruin everything."

She was shaking by the time she got back in her

bedroom, shaking so hard she collapsed on the tufted slipper chair. Outside the sun was shining, inside she was still desperately cold. She wrapped her arms around her body, rocking back and forth. There had to be some way out of this mess. Without sacrificing her sister. Mother. Whatever.

God, she felt like something out of *Chinatown.* The thought should have amused her, but right now her sense of humor seemed to have vanished. She felt trapped, smothered, with no way out. Even Jack McGowan, for all his dire warnings, hadn't offered any possibility of escape.

There had to be a way out. There was a reason she was here, or at least was dreaming she was here, and it couldn't be to repeat history. That much was absolutely certain.

She looked at her reflection in the hinged mirror over the kidney-shaped dressing table. Tallulah Abbott was pale, her dark brown eyes haunted, her full, unpainted mouth faintly tremulous. She bit her lip, favoring the stranger in the mirror with her steeliest expression, and was pleased to see that Lou Abbott could look surprisingly stern despite her lush beauty.

She could see the faint bloodstain Jack had told her about, and she touched it. Putting on that shirt had felt like sliding into a warm embrace, and now she knew why. Tallulah had obviously cherished that shirt, and it might simply be because it was loose and comfortable, unlike the rest of her fussy and tailored clothes.

But Susan didn't think so. Lou treasured it because it had belonged to Jack McGowan. He'd taken the shirt off his back and wrapped her in it, long ago, and somewhere in this stranger's body she could still remember how wonderful it felt.

But Jack wasn't the answer. He didn't want her, he'd never wanted her. She was like a kid sister, his brother's girl, someone he kissed for God-only-knew-what reason, but not someone he wanted. He was leaving, and he was leaving her behind.

She stripped off the shirt and threw it in the frilly wastebasket. She could already see fresh marks on her skin where Neddie had bruised her, and she shivered again. She wasn't going to submit tamely to their plans for her. And she found it equally hard to believe that Tallulah had submitted.

Susan hadn't the faintest idea how she was supposed to arrange her hair, what kind of makeup she was supposed to wear. All the lipsticks were bright, intense colors, and the mascara came in a tiny little compact with a separate brush. She could tell that Lou's eyebrows had been carefully plucked, and her hair was dark enough that she shouldn't need to use eyebrow pencil. Not unless she was supposed to look like Joan Crawford, and with any luck 1949 was too late for the skinny eyebrow look. She was forced to succumb to the girdle again—as far as she could tell there was no other way to hold up the seamed stockings. She was standing inside the closet door, staring at the possibilities, when she smelled the fresh cigarette smoke. She jumped back, startled, to face Elda.

Her mother's stepmother looked like the very picture of a jaded woman, from her bloodred fingernails to the cigarette drooping from her coral lips. If Elda was anything to go by, the Joan Crawford *Mommie Dearest* style was still alive and kicking.

"I hear you upset Neddie this morning," she said, moving into the bedroom and closing the door behind her. "I thought you were smarter than that. Neddie's easy enough to handle if you know how. You can't threaten him or push him. He likes sweet, fluttery little girls who hang on his every word. That's your role, darling. I thought you knew how to play it."

Susan didn't move, keeping her expression blank as she listened for clues. What was up between the two of them?

"I don't want to marry him," she said flatly.

Elda's smile was faint and unsurprised. "Of course you don't. You've already told us that. And we've told you that you don't have a choice. He'll ruin us if you don't."

"This is like some bad Hollywood movie."

"You should know, sweetie. You've always been addicted to them, like some shopgirl from the five-and-dime. People like the Abbotts don't go rushing to matinees, they don't marry for love, they don't disobey their parents or their husbands. They know what's expected of them in this life."

"And what's expected of me?"

"You don't need me to remind you, Lou. You know perfectly well that without Neddie's support your father will lose everything. This house, what little money we have left, the respect of the community. He'd probably kill himself if any of his little dabblings were made public. You wouldn't want that on your conscience, now would you?"

Susan had never before looked in the face of pure evil, and the effect was disturbing. Elda blew a perfect smoke ring, and her coral lips curved in a catlike smile. "Of course you wouldn't." She answered the question for herself. "Are you afraid of sex, sweetie? I gather you kept yourself charmingly pure for your long-lost soldier boy, and I know that no one's been around since, except for Jack McGowan, and you haven't had the chance to let him under your skirts. I can't really set your mind at ease about Neddie. He's quite a demanding lover, and probably not well-suited for a virgin. By the time you're experienced enough to enjoy him, he'll probably lose interest, but then, no one has any right to expect a happy ending, do they?" She crossed the room and stubbed out her cigarette on the glass-topped dressing table. "Let me give you a little hint. Some motherly advice on the eve of your wedding. If you're sweet and shy and demure and do everything he orders you to do he probably won't hurt you as much as he would if you fight him. But if you fight back, make him force you, it will excite him so much he'll finish even more quickly. It's up to you, my pet. If you want the pain and humiliation over quickly or if you're willing to endure for the chance of it not hurting quite so much.''

Susan stared at her, aghast. ''You sound like something out of a Victorian novel,'' she said. ''Sex isn't humiliating and painful.''

Elda smiled. ''It is with Neddie. Quite enjoyably so. I speak from experience.''

Susan stared at her in stricken horror, but Elda ignored her, pushing her out of the way to rifle through her closet. She pulled out a fluttery peach-flowered dress and shoved it at her. ''Put this one on, dear, and fix your makeup. You look like a ghost. The wedding party is starting to arrive, Cousin Doug is already loaded, and Ginny is too busy with that little brat of hers to keep him away from the bar. You'd think she'd know better than to bring a baby to a wedding rehearsal, but she never had much sense.''

Susan caught the dress in her arms, still unable to say a word. ''And smile, damn it,'' Elda hissed, all her false affability vanishing. ''Look like you're divinely happy and desperately in love. Just pretend you're marrying Jack.''

That roused her. ''Jack?'' Tallulah's husky voice sounded almost raw coming from her throat.

''You think I don't know? You've had a crush on that man as long as I've known you. You only got engaged to Jimmy because you accepted the fact that you couldn't have him, and then my, oh, my, didn't you feel guilty when Jimmy died? You still can't have Jack, and you still want him. So just look up at Neddie and pretend he's Jack. It might even work in bed, at least for a while, though their styles are completely different.''

"You slept with Jack?" Susan demanded, horrified.

"A long, long time ago, precious. And very guilty he was about it. He didn't realize I wasn't about to let him say no. He's good, I have to admit. But not nearly as willing to play my little games as Neddie is.'' She leaned over and gave Susan a cool, dry kiss on her cheek. "Too bad you'll never have a chance to compare them, darling.''

"'And here's to you, Mrs. Robinson,''' Susan muttered underneath her breath.

"The strong flourish, darling. The weak fade away, which will be your fate, I'm afraid. At least you can cherish your martyrdom, knowing that you did it all for your darling little sister. And she'll never have the faintest idea you weren't a divinely happy bride, will she?''

Perhaps Tallulah accepted her fate. But Elda didn't know she was dealing with a nineties woman. She met Elda's supercilious smirk with a faint smile of her own. "I'll be down as soon as I'm dressed.''

For a moment Elda's complacency faded. "You are going to be sensible, aren't you?''

Susan turned away, unwilling to let her see her expression. "How well do you know me, Elda?"

"That's not an answer."

"It's all you're going to get. If you expect me to come down in time for the rehearsal you'd be smart to leave me alone. I've had quite enough upset for one morning."

"Poor little bride," Elda laughed, her equanimity restored. "I'll go down and entertain the men for you. But don't keep them waiting too long. You know about Neddie's temper." She touched the bruising on Susan's arms.

The door closed behind her, leaving Susan standing in the middle of the room, trembling with anger. "I know Neddie's temper," she murmured. "But you don't know Susan Abbott."

And she moved back to the dressing table, rejecting the pastel pink lipstick and colored her mouth a bright, wicked red. War paint, she thought. Ready for battle.

Chapter Eleven

The wedding rehearsal was an absolute nightmare. St. Anne's Episcopal Church hadn't changed in fifty years, and for the first time Susan found herself in familiar territory. It was both comforting and eerie, and she would have liked nothing more than to slip into one of the wooden pews for a few solitary minutes and see if she could find the answers in what was certainly a logical place to look for them.

When she suggested she might like a few moments of quiet prayer Tallulah's father and fiancé looked at her as if she was possessed. "No need for such nonsense," Ridley dismissed it in his gruff voice. "You'll have plenty of time for that once you're married."

"You're not going to become some kind of religious fanatic, are you?" Neddie demanded.

"Wanting to pray would make me a religious fanatic?"

"Please!" Ridley said. "Religion is a personal

matter, not for public discussion. For heaven's sake spare us your insights.''

So much for spiritual help, Susan thought. The rehearsal went on and on and on, the old stone church filled with chattering people she had to pretend to know. Fortunately Mary kept close, whispering identifications in her ear, and Susan managed to keep a straight face when she'd meet someone she'd heretofore known as a stately dowager.

The dead ones were the hardest. Susan's mother had been instilled with proper social etiquette, and when an Abbott family friend or distant relative had died she had considered it her duty to attend the funeral, and quite often she'd taken her daughter with her, training Susan in the fine art of social niceties. There were at least a dozen hale, hearty, jovial members of the massive wedding party whom Susan had seen buried, and kissing their warm cheeks, smiling at them while she knew their eventual fate, was completely unnerving.

There were ten bridesmaids, all chattering in high-pitched voices, but for some reason her godmother, Louisa, wasn't among them. There were ten ushers, their deeper voices echoing in counterpoint in the old stone church. The priest, Father Montgomery, was a stately old man whose mellow tones could barely be heard above the babble, and the organist forgot to show up. Someone else pitched in with a mistake-ridden version of the bridal march, and Susan had no choice but to let Ridley drag her up the aisle on her tottery high heels, following the bevy of chattering debutantes, to hand her over to Neddie.

Jack stood next to him, and Susan stared up in utter horror, ignoring her fiancé. "You're the best man?"

"Don't be an idiot, Tallulah," Neddie snapped. "You know perfectly well Freddy is the best man. McGowan is just filling in until he gets here."

"Kind of you," she murmured dazedly.

"Let's get this over with," Ridley announced. "The rest of the family is expecting us back at the house for the rehearsal dinner."

The bridesmaids bumped into each other. Ridley tripped as he practiced moving back to the front pew. The ushers kept losing their places, and Neddie stepped on her foot when they practiced kneeling at the altar.

But worst of all, Jack McGowan refused to mimic the best man's part in the ceremony. "I forgot the ring," he said, his hands shoved carelessly in his pockets.

Neddie growled, but Father Montgomery simply laughed. "It's lucky you're only standing in, young man, or we would have a disaster on our hands."

"People can get married without a ring," Neddie rumbled. "I don't intend to let anything get in the way of this ceremony." He smiled his flashing smile, and it seemed as if no one else heard the threat in his voice.

By the time they all piled back into the various

cars, the noise level had risen to an even shriller pitch, and Susan's head was aching so badly she wanted to scream. On the way over to the church she'd been crammed into a huge black sedan, wedged between bridesmaids. Neddie was in the midst of hustling her toward that same sedan when she spied a wonderful-looking hot rod belonging to one of the younger ushers.

Mary was already ensconced in the back seat of the convertible, squeezed between two of the ushers, looking absolutely delighted. "Come with us, Lou!" she called. "You need the wind in your hair."

Neddie's fingers dug painfully into her arm, but there was no way he could stop her without making a scene. "I'd love to," she called, pulling away from him and running across the neatly manicured lawn. She climbed into the front seat, flashing her sister a brilliant smile. At the moment nothing mattered more than simply getting away from Neddie's oppressive presence.

"You used to love fast cars. You wanna drive, Lou?" the young man behind the wheel asked, and for a moment Susan was sorely tempted. But she'd never learned to operate a standard shift, and God only knew what kind of clutch and choke these old cars had.

"You drive," she said airily. "I'll enjoy the ride."

The young man took off with a squeal of tires, throwing Susan back against the seat, and she heard Mary shriek with laughter.

"What are you looking for?" the driver shouted over the rushing wind.

Susan stopped rummaging around her. Of course there'd be no seat belt. And there was nothing to worry about—in 1999 Mary was still alive and Tallulah had survived long enough to marry Neddie. "I dropped a...a bobby pin," she said, feeling very clever.

"You don't use bobby pins, Lou!" Mary called from the back seat. "Hey, Todd, why don't we drive to Eddie's and get some ice cream?"

"Aren't we supposed to be back for the dinner?"

"They'll start without us. I need ice cream," she shouted.

"Sounds good to me."

Susan sat very still in the front seat. "Todd?" she said.

He was a gorgeous young man, healthy, full of high spirits and gentle humor, and Susan had a sudden dreadful feeling she knew exactly who he was. Her mother had told her about their beloved cousin Todd, who'd died in a car accident when he was in his early twenties. The young man beside her drove fast and well, and his smile was full of charm as he switched on the car radio and filled the air with music.

She leaned over and turned the sound down. "Todd," she said again, her voice urgent.

"What, Lou?" He caught the seriousness of her voice, and he slowed the car a bit.

"Drive carefully."

He grinned. "Don't worry, cuz. I'm not going to crack us up the night before your wedding. Trust me. I can't imagine why you're so eager to marry someone like old Neddie, but it's your choice. I won't do anything to stop you."

"Oh, feel free," she said airily.

"I wouldn't want to interfere with fate." He pulled up to a drive-in ice-cream stand with a flourish.

She remembered his grave in the family plot near her grandfather's. He'd died in the early 1950s, his car going off a bridge in Princeton when he was an undergraduate. "I would," she said firmly. "Too many people die in car accidents. Slow down."

"I'm parked, Lou!"

"I mean in general," she said. "Especially on bridges. Promise me."

He grinned at her, a charming, youthful grin. "You're nuts, you know that?"

"Promise me. As a wedding present."

He shook his head with a rueful laugh. "I promise, Lou. I'll drive like a parson."

It was the best she could hope for. She could still see the marble headstone, one Abbott amidst so many other Abbotts, and then a sudden realization struck her.

Tallulah's grave wasn't in that large, dignified family plot. Her parents were there, cousins, aunts, uncles, grandparents and great-grandparents and even beyond. Susan had been there just last year, as Great-aunt Tessie had been interred.

But there was no stone marking Tallulah Abbott's final resting place.

Without thinking she turned to Mary. "Where did they bury Tallulah?"

For a moment a shocked silence filled the car. Then Todd laughed. "Beneath Neddie, I expect. But you're going to have to wait a few decades."

Susan managed an airy laugh, and the tension was broken. "Sorry, I must have been daydreaming. Thinking about death, I'm afraid."

"You're supposed to be thinking about the future," Mary said sternly.

"Well, eventually that'll be the future. Where do you want to be buried?"

"Ewwww," Mary said with a grimace. "Listen, the family plot by St. Anne's is big enough for every Abbott whoever lived. We'll all be there."

Except Tallulah.

"Let's concentrate on what's important," one of boys in the back said. "Ice cream."

"You'll have chocolate, right, Lou?" Mary prompted her. "You've always been crazy about chocolate."

Susan hated chocolate. Her mother had always insisted she had to be a changeling—no Abbott woman had ever failed to be a total chocoholic. Though in fact, that was exactly what she was at the moment. A changeling.

"I think I'll have black raspberry instead," she said. "After all, I'm starting a new life tomorrow, I might as well begin now by trying new things."

"Will wonders never cease? Tallulah Abbott turning down chocolate!" The older boy in the back, a young man named Wilson, collapsed in mock surprise.

Susan grinned at him. Wilson grew up to father one of her best friends, and he'd always been one of her favorite people. "Life is full of surprises, Wilson," she said. "You couldn't even begin to guess."

The party was in full swing by the time they made it back to the Abbott mansion. Elda and Ridley had seen to everything—the catering trucks were parked off to one side, and several uniformed young men were parking the myriad of classic vehicles. Except they weren't classic—most of them were brand-spanking-new, the product of postwar production.

Susan looked about her dazedly as she climbed the wide front steps. "How many people are here?"

"You know Elda." Mary was by her side. "She loves to put on a party. Let's just hope everyone's in a good mood and we don't have any disasters."

"I think that's too much to hope for," Susan muttered, taking a deep breath and stepping into the noisy crowd.

It was. The wicked trio, Elda, Ridley and Neddie were holding court, each with their own coterie, and all three fixed Susan with a steely glare when she made her belated entrance. Fortunately the party was so crowded there was no way any of them could get close enough to make their displeasure known, and she simply smiled, said all the right things to perfect strangers and moved on out to the formal gardens. Long tables had been set up out there, covered in white linen and silver chafing dishes. Even eating al fresco the Abbotts did things in a grand manner. Most of the younger people were outside, and even though no one loosened a tie or slipped off a high-heeled shoe, they seemed relatively at ease.

The back gardens abutted on a thick forest that in fifty years would be upscale condos. Right now it was an artfully wild tangle of growth, marking the border where the Abbotts could no longer control things, though there were paths leading through the woods, and several couples were already taking advantage of them. It was a warmish night, though Susan couldn't rid herself of that lingering chill that had plagued her for what seemed like forever. She ought to go back in the house and see if she could find a cardigan or something, but then she'd run the risk of running into her fiancé and her parents, and a little chill was worth a few minutes' peace.

There were a few children around—a couple of preadolescent girls trying hard to be grown-up, a towheaded toddler, just barely walking, wandering around with her harassed mother trailing behind her. The noise by the outside bar was getting louder, the laughter growing, as the early evening darkened around them.

Fortunately Mary had raised her with all the necessary social skills of an earlier generation. She was entirely capable of holding long conversations with total strangers she supposedly had known her entire life, asking the right questions, nodding sagely, smiling, smiling. She wanted to get away from them all. If one more slightly inebriated young man came up to her and offered to steal her away from Neddie, if one more young woman sighed over how lucky she was to have won someone who was handsome, wealthy and charming, she would scream.

Cousin Ginny, chasing her rambunctious baby, passed by. "I just wanted to tell you how lucky you are," she said breathlessly, as her little one toddled on by. "Neddie's absolutely wonderful. I'm hoping he can get your cousin Doug a job."

Mary had already primed her on this one—Doug was a drinker, Ginny his long-suffering wife, and between the two of them they didn't have a cent. Only baby Krissie wandering around, grabbing food off the table and chortling.

"I'm sure he will," Susan said. "Excuse me, Ginny, I'll be right back." And she practically sprinted toward the edge of the garden, or as close to sprinting as she could go in the high-heeled, open-toed shoes she was wearing.

The crowds thinned out by the edge of the woods, and she paused, taking a deep breath. The terrace was packed with people, and she could see Neddie now, looking around him impatiently. She was too far away to see his expression, but his body language was easy enough to read. He was looking for his errant bride, and he wasn't pleased with her.

She wasn't in the mood to be manhandled, lectured or even glowered at. There was no one nearby, and she simply melted into the woods before anyone could notice she was gone.

Or so she hoped. It was still and quiet in the forest. In the distance she could hear music and the chattering voices. A band had set up on the west side of the lawn—Mary was right in that Elda spared no expense when she entertained. But the tall trees and shrubbery muffled the noise, and as the darkness descended she could see a few fireflies flickering about.

She couldn't very well sit in her damned fussy frock, so she leaned against a thick tree and closed her eyes, breathing in the cool air, the deceptive stillness, with that foreign world she'd landed in remote and set apart. If she tried very hard she could almost feel as if she were home again.

She lost track of time, her eyes closed, dreaming, when she suddenly realized she wasn't alone in her little clearing in the woods. Someone was watching her.

If she ignored him maybe he'd go away. It couldn't be Neddie—he'd barge up and grab her, not keep his distance. And it couldn't be Ridley—he'd be whining. As far as she could figure out, there was only one person in 1949 Matchfield, Connecticut, who'd be interested enough to follow her. And he was standing too damned close.

She opened her eyes, staring up into Jack's somber ones. "Are you stalking me?"

"Stalking?" he echoed, perplexed.

They didn't have *stalkers* in the past? "Never mind," she said. "What did you want? I was looking for a little peace and quiet, not cozy conversation."

It was darker now, the lights from the patio a distant glow. The music was growing louder, and people were dancing.

"The conversation I had in mind isn't particularly cozy," he said.

"What now? More dire warnings? Why don't you pull out all the stops and tell me Jimmy would be spinning in his grave if he knew I was going to marry Neddie Marsden? You've tried everything else."

"You think he'd approve?"

"Of course not. But Jimmy's dead, we both know that. And I can't live my life the way he would have wanted."

"Yes, you can."

"And how do you suggest I do that?"

"You could come away with me instead of marrying that bastard."

She slapped him. Hard, across the face, hurting her hand, the sound of it shocking. And then she stood frozen, disbelieving that she had done such a thing.

He didn't react. "You've seen too many Hollywood movies, Lou," he said in a caustic voice.

"I—I'm sorry…"

"No, don't apologize. It ruins the entire effect," he drawled. "Outraged womanhood and all that. How come a proposal deserves a slap, though? Outside of the fact that it's the night before your wedding to someone else."

"It wasn't a proposal and you know it."

"Sounded like one to me."

"So you followed me into the woods during my rehearsal dinner to propose...something. Any particular reason? Were you suddenly overcome by passion? You realized you've loved me forever and you can't see me throwing my life away on the wrong man?"

He said nothing, the mark of her hand standing out against his tanned face.

"What, no passionate declarations of love?" she mocked him. "Of course not. You see, I know why you're doing this, Jack. It was Jimmy's idea, right? It just took you four years to get around to it," she said bitterly. She was beyond thinking clearly, beyond wondering how she knew things only Tallulah would know. Somehow during the past forty-eight hours she and Lou had become one, and Lou's emotions and memories had become hers. The man in front of her, the man she wanted to kill, was the man she was in love with, and always had been.

"It was Jimmy's idea," Jack said finally. "He must have known there was a good chance he wouldn't come back. He wrote and asked me to look after you."

"Well, I'd say you failed, big-time," she shot back. "You blew your brother's last request, hotshot. I'm being forced to marry a bullying criminal, and there's not a damned thing anyone can do about it. And your noble sacrifice is too damned little, too damned late."

To her amazement he didn't look particularly chastened. As a matter of fact, he smiled at her, with something like relief. "That's the Lou I remember," he said. "For four years you've been walking around like a zombie. I don't think you let a curse word past your lips in all that time. Welcome back."

"Go to hell."

"You want to hit me again?" he taunted.

"Yes!" She moved toward him, like a fool, not realizing his intention. He caught her upraised hand and pulled her into his arms, her body slamming up against his. This time when he kissed her she kissed him back, surrendering with a quiet moan of longing and despair.

It went on forever. His big hands threaded through her carefully arranged hair, pulling it free, and he kissed her mouth, her throat, the corners of her eyes.

"Run away with me, Lou," he whispered against her skin. "We can make a good team. We're both too old to believe in true love anymore...."

She kicked him. Hard, in the shins, her uncomfortable shoes finally good for something.

"I repeat. Go...to...hell." And she strode off down the path to the party, her back straight, bristling with fury.

Chapter Twelve

Susan was so intent on escaping from Jack that she failed to notice someone looming up at the edge of the woods, and it was too late to avoid barreling into them. At least it wasn't Neddie or Ridley.

Unfortunately it was Elda.

She caught Susan by the arms, inadvertently squeezing where Neddie had already bruised her. "Where are you running off to, precious?" she purred. "The blushing bride is the center of the party, and no one's been able to find you for ages."

"Did they really notice?"

"No," Elda said with an airy laugh. "But I did. I was worried you might be trying to run away. You've always had an almost saintlike sense of responsibility, but I know the lure of an attractive young man, and it's common knowledge you've always been desperately in love with Jack McGowan. Is that who you were meeting in the woods?"

"I didn't meet anyone in the woods."

"You look well kissed, and I'm a woman who

knows the look. If it were anyone else I'd say you'd been doing a lot more than that, but we know Saint Lou is planning on being a martyred virgin bride, so she's unlikely to indulge in a little prenuptial hanky-panky. So tell me, did Jack pledge his undying love?''

Susan was tired, frustrated and angry. She looked at the smug, elegant woman who was taunting her, and something snapped. "Doesn't this wicked step-mother thing get a little old after a while, Elda?" she drawled.

She'd managed to startle Elda out of her mocking complacency. "Have you developed claws, my dear? It's a little late for that. Your fate is sealed."

"Lord, Elda, what kind of books do you read? My fate is sealed? Don't be ridiculous," Susan snapped.

Elda was looking at her as if she'd suddenly sprouted horns and a tail. "It's a little late to regrow your backbone. You aren't thinking of backing out of our agreement, are you? The family—"

"The family is counting on me, yes, I know," Susan said. "If I don't marry Neddie the family is disgraced and ruined, including my little sister. It sounds like something out of a melodrama."

"Life can be very melodramatic. And you forgot one important point. Your father's being investigated by the government, and I'm afraid his...involvement in the issue of faulty machinery was a bit more than Neddie's. Neddie has been covering up for him, but the price must be paid. And you, my dear, are going to pay it.''

She'd heard the phrase, having one's blood run cold, but she'd never actually experienced it before. ''What exactly did my father do? Did people die because of Ridley's greed? Did soldiers die?''

''Soldiers always die, and greed is always part of the cause. Grow up, Tallulah. Time to put away childish things like idealism and get on with life. It's almost the 1950s. Time to face the future.''

Face the future. Save Tallulah. Protect her mother. Stop the wedding. The choices flew at her head like crazed bats, and she wanted to strike at them, driving them away.

''Message received, Elda,'' she said calmly. ''What are you doing out here besides delivering dire warnings? Were you looking for me?''

''Actually I'd forgotten. Cousin Ginny's misplaced her ridiculous baby. You'd think she'd know infants aren't welcome at a social occasion like this, but people are so selfish,'' she said with an absolutely straight face, the epitome of self-absorption. ''If anything happens to that child I'll be devastated!''

Susan blinked. ''You will?''

''We'd have to postpone the wedding.''

''Would we?'' It was only momentarily tempting. She could bribe Hattie to take the baby off for a couple of days. Or bribe Ginny, whose heavy-drinking husband seemed to be causing all sorts of financial woes.

Nice idea, but impractical. She couldn't save Tallulah's butt by risking a baby's security. "I'll go look for her," she said wearily, starting back toward the woods.

Elda grabbed her arm, swinging her around. "No, you won't," she said flatly. "You'll go back inside the house and keep Neddie company. You've been ignoring him all evening, and we don't want people to get the wrong idea, now do we?"

"That we don't actually like each other? Heavens, why would they think that?" Susan said in a mocking voice. "Why isn't Neddie looking for the baby?"

"He isn't the outdoors type. Besides, everyone else is searching madly—there's no need for him to bother himself."

"He's all heart, isn't he?"

"He's a determined man, Tallulah. Don't make the mistake of underestimating him. He'll win."

"So he tells me," Susan said. "That doesn't mean he'll win without a fight." She yanked her arm free, turning her back on the house and her fiancé. Heading into the gathering darkness, in search of a lost child.

The night grew still and dark around the sprawling Abbott mansion. Even the band members had abandoned their instruments to join in the search for the missing child, and the night air echoed with a myriad of voices, calling the baby's name.

She wasn't afraid to go back into the woods, wasn't afraid that she might run into Jack again, with his seductive mouth and his clueless soul. Neddie might sit in comfort while a child was missing—Jack would do no such thing. He'd be off searching as well, and whatever complicated agenda drove him would be superseded by the greater need.

Apart from the fact that he seemed to have no idea that Lou Abbott was desperately in love with him, he was everything a hero should be.

Odd, that whenever he touched her she didn't feel like Susan anymore. The past, or was it the future, faded, and she became Tallulah, completely, body and soul.

But he didn't recognize that they belonged together. He didn't believe in love or happy endings, and she wasn't sure she could blame him. If she'd had to go through a war she might not believe in happy endings, either.

The night grew thick and dark around her, the lights from the house warring with the newly risen moon. The distant cries had faded, and she could hear the soft strains of music from the band once more. She looked down at the thin watch on her wrist, but she'd forgotten she had to wind the stupid thing, and it had stopped hours ago, probably during the rehearsal.

She wondered whether the baby had been found, or whether Elda had simply decreed that a party was more important than a lost child.

She skirted the edge of the lawn, staying out of the glare of lights, and went into the house through the French doors on the lower level, hoping to avoid Neddie. She found herself in the deserted library, lit only by the faint glow of a desk lamp that spread a pool of light throughout the walnut-paneled room.

She wasn't alone. Someone was sitting in the darkness, a mere shadow in the cavernous room, and she started to tiptoe out when the oddly familiar sound of heavy breathing stopped her in her tracks.

She took a few tentative steps toward the sofa, her eyes accustomed to the dim light, and then stopped. Her instincts had been right—Jack McGowan sat sprawled on the sofa, sound asleep. With a towheaded baby nestled comfortably against his shoulder.

He was snoring softly, which didn't seem to disturb the sleeping baby one bit. He'd loosened his tie, his hair was ruffled and he was in need of a shave. He was the best thing she'd ever seen in her life.

She could see the mark of her hand where she'd slapped him, just faintly against the tanned skin. She let herself linger on his mouth, which had kissed her with such devastating tenderness.

With an instinct that belonged to someone else, she sank into a chair behind her, one she hadn't even seen in the first place, and stared at him. It was sentiment, of course. There was nothing sexier than a big strong man cradling a helpless baby—she'd seen enough perfume ads to know it.

But this was before the time of evocative perfume ads. This was a man who'd simply gone out and found the missing baby, no muss, no fuss. The kind of man a baby trusts instinctively.

Shouldn't she trust him, as well?

She looked at him, and knew she loved him. She didn't even know who or what she was anymore, but she loved the man sprawled on the sofa with a baby in his arms, and would love him until she died.

She shut her eyes, fighting the tears that wanted to squeeze past. She was so tired, so uncertain. She felt more lost than the baby who lay snuggled against McGowan. And she knew, instinctively, that that was where she belonged. Sleeping safely in his arms, home at last.

She swallowed the tears determinedly. Neither Lou nor Susan Abbott were the kind of women who cried easily, and they weren't about to start now. She opened her eyes, to find Jack was watching her.

"You found Krissie," she whispered.

"It was easy enough, if you know kids. I've got a bunch of nieces and nephews, and besides, I like them. I know how their minds work."

"Does anyone know you found her?"

"Her mother does. She's busy dealing with her husband at the moment. The rest of the guests lost interest in the search."

"Pigs," she said.

"Yeah." The baby shifted on his chest, making soft, snuffling noises.

"I'm sorry I hit you," she said after a moment.

"Hey, I'm sure I deserved it. As a matter of fact, anytime I get slapped it's probably long overdue."

Another silence fell between them, oddly comfortable. "You'll make a good father," she said. "Babies trust you."

"Dogs do, too," he murmured wryly.

"I want lots of children." She didn't know where that came from, but it popped into her brain and onto her tongue.

"I'm sure Neddie will be more than happy to oblige," he drawled. "And he'll have plenty of money to support you and your brood. Of course, I can't vouch for what your children will be like. If they're half Neddie then the prospect isn't too encouraging. I hate to think of this world being populated by more Neddie Marsdens."

"Why do you hate him so much?"

He looked at her across the tousled white-blond curls of the sleeping child. "He's a war profiteer, making money off the blood of dying soldiers. He's a peace profiteer, putting up tacky, shoddily made houses for people who deserve better. He's a bully with a mean, sharp, narrow mind, and he's everything that's bad about this country. But that's not why I hate him."

"Then why?"

"Because of what he'll do to you. He'll take every spark of life out of you, he'll turn you into some kind of perfect wife, and everything you ever were or cared about will be lost. You'll be as dead as Jimmy. And I don't want to see that."

"You won't be seeing it, remember? You're going back overseas."

"Yeah," he said. "As a matter of fact, I decided I'd had about enough of these festivities. I figured I owed it to Jimmy to warn you, and if you didn't listen at least to see you married in style. But I changed my mind. I can't stand by and watch you throw your life away, not after so many people lost theirs. I'm leaving tomorrow before the wedding. I'm due in Singapore by mid-July, and it's gonna take me a while to get there. There's no reason to put off going. Unless you can give me one."

She could, a powerful one. Though whether he would want to be passionately loved by Lou Abbott was another question entirely.

But it wasn't up to her. Not until she made sure Mary was safe.

She rose, crossing the shadow-filled room. In the distance the band played "Sentimental Journey." In the room the baby slept on Jack McGowan's chest, her tiny fist caught in his rumpled white shirt.

"Do you want a reason?" she asked him in a level voice.

"No."

His answer surprised her. He looked wary, almost afraid, and she never thought Jack would be afraid of anything.

"Why not?"

He took a deep breath. "Do you know what guilt is, Lou? How it crawls onto your back, digs its talons into you and holds on, draining everything from you? It's a vampire, sucking away life and happiness and hope. It's no way to live. And that's what kills me about Marsden. He deserves to be writhing in the flames of hell for what he did, and he's going to spend his days rich and comfortable."

"What have you got to feel guilty for?"

"A million things...nothing at all. You don't need to hear my confession, Lou. I'm going to Singapore, not dying. And my sins aren't all that unusual."

"What are they? Did you do something cowardly during the war? It's nothing to be ashamed of— you're only human. Everyone gets scared sometimes."

"I was scared spitless most of the time, Lou, but no, I didn't do anything cowardly. Besides, I was a war correspondent—my job was to report, not to kill. It made things easier. Maybe."

"Or maybe it made things harder," she said, kneeling down by the sofa. She needed to touch him. She didn't want to wake the baby, but she needed to feel the warmth of his flesh beneath her hand. She was so cold, so very cold.

"So why the guilt, Jack? If it was guilt that you didn't kill people, get over it."

She startled a reluctant grin from him. "No, it's not guilt that I didn't kill people. I'm damned grateful I don't have to live with that."

"Then what is it?"

"None of your damned—"

"I need to know, Jack. Don't you think you owe me that much?" She wasn't sure how he'd react. She wasn't sure why she thought he owed her anything, or why he might think he did.

"Jimmy's dead," he said finally, "and I'm alive."

His bleak tone silenced her for a moment. "Survivor's guilt," she said finally. "It's understandable..."

"Spare me that crap," he said harshly, never raising his voice. "I could live with Jimmy's death. I lost too damned many friends as it is, and I can live with it."

"Then what's the problem?"

"I can't live with wanting Jimmy's girl. I won't take what he can't have, I won't steal his happy ending."

She sat back on her heels, staring at him. "You sexist pig," she muttered.

"What?"

"Obviously you've never heard that term before," she said caustically. "If you weren't running away, I'd give you plenty of chances to get used to it."

"What are you so mad about?" he snapped. "I just told you I...wanted you. You should be flattered."

"Flattered that you're lusting after me? Thanks, but I've got a mirror. Tallulah Abbott is definitely lust-worthy material—why do you think Neddie wants to marry her?'' She didn't stop to consider how odd that sounded, referring to Lou in the third person.

She rose to her full height, the high heels killing her ankles, and stared down at him in cool disdain. ''What I object to is you considering me some sort of war trophy. To the victor goes the spoils—at least, to the survivor. I'm not someone to be passed around to the most deserving war hero, dead or alive. I'm not a household decoration, I'm not a teenage sweetheart, I'm not a madonna and I'm damned well not a whore. I'm a woman, Jack McGowan. My own person, belonging to no one. A woman with brains and talents and needs and love. And I don't care how guilty you feel—you can learn to live with it. You can learn to live with—''

''There you are!'' Cousin Ginny, harassed and grateful, rushed into the room, stopping her in the midst of her declaration. ''I can't thank you enough for watching Krissie for me, Jack. I was so terrified when I couldn't find her, and no one else seemed to care.'' She reached down and carefully scooped the sleeping baby from Jack's chest and tucked her in her arms. The baby slept on, dead to the world.

''They cared, Ginny,'' he said gently, pushing himself off the sofa. ''I'm just a little better at finding lost souls.''

She wanted to escape. It was one thing, looming over him as he lay sprawled on the sofa, another to have him on his feet, towering over her. Making her feel small and needy, reminding her of how vulnerable she was. To him. Ginny was still babbling her thanks, blocking the doorway to the rest of the house, but the terrace door was still open, and she took a surreptitious step backward. He moved around the mother and child quite deftly, catching her arm before she could make her escape.

Everyone was always putting their hands on her. But it was only Jack's hands that felt gentle, comforting. The others were trying to grab her, force her to do what they wanted. Jack's hands were strong but tender. Forcing her to do what she wanted.

And then Ginny and her baby were gone, and she was alone with him in the darkness. "I can learn to live with what, Lou?" he said softly.

In the distance she could hear Neddie's voice, loud and blustery, and Elda's musical laugh. The band was playing "Night and Day," and she wanted to moan in protest. There was something undeniably erotic about "Night and Day," and she'd never been able to resist it.

She said nothing, staring up at him in the darkness, wanting him so badly her knees felt weak.

"I can learn to live without you?"

She didn't say anything. She couldn't. He reached up and cupped her face, tilting her head back. She could feel tears slipping beneath her closed eyelids, and she held her breath, waiting, her heart pounding, waiting, needing, wanting.

She felt his thumbs brush her tears. The almost imperceptible brush of his lips against hers. "I guess I'll have to," he whispered.

And she was alone.

Chapter Thirteen

The next morning dawned bright and clear. The morning of Tallulah Abbott's wedding. The morning of the last day of her life, unless she could change history. She lay very still in bed, her eyes tightly shut. She had no illusions that she'd somehow managed to return to her own time and place. The bed beneath her was still too soft, the smell of cigarettes in the air was inescapable, and the bias-cut silk nightgown had slid around her body into an awkward, binding position.

Still, if she didn't open her eyes she could put off the strange mutated reality a little bit longer. It didn't have to be her wedding day. The day she was going to die.

At that dismal thought her eyes flew open against her will. "It's not your wedding day," she said out loud. "It's Tallulah's. She's the one who's marrying the wrong man, she's the one who's supposed to die."

And she was the one who was supposed to somehow stop it. What would happen if she didn't? Would she die, as well, or would she simply be flung back into her own life? Did her own survival depend upon changing history? Or if she changed it, would she be stuck in it? Was this where she really belonged?

There were two people inside her body right now. Or inside Lou's body. Her soul and Tallulah Abbott's were inextricably entwined—she no longer knew which emotions were hers and which were Lou's. Which were her memories and which belonged to her long-dead aunt.

Somehow she had become Lou, in heart and soul as well as body. Susan was disappearing, fading away, like morning mist when its greeted by a fiery sunrise. And there was nothing she could do about it. Nothing she wanted to do about it.

There were other, more important issues to deal with on today of all days. It was just after seven in the morning, according to the loudly ticking alarm clock that was set to go off in another half an hour. Tallulah Abbott was due to marry Edward Marsden in an elaborate ceremony at St. Anne's Church at eleven o'clock this morning. If she was going to salvage the situation she'd better get going instead of lazing in bed pondering two women's futures.

Mary Abbott was the key to it all. When it came right down to it, it was the children who mattered. Not just because they were the future. But because they couldn't look after themselves, not completely. Someone had to be looking after them, and it was unlikely that either Elda or Ridley Abbott gave a damn about a nine-year-old girl's future.

The baggy dungarees and Jack's white shirt still hung in her closet. She was half-surprised that Elda hadn't sent someone in to remove the clothing on Neddie's orders, but they were still there, still the most comfortable thing she owned. It felt different, pulling Jack's shirt around her body, knowing it was his. Feeling it like an embrace. She did it, anyway, this time not even bothering with sneakers, heading out into the early-morning chill barefoot and ready.

Mary's room was empty. Her bed had been slept in, her striped pajamas lay in a heap on the floor, a sight which amused Susan. How many times had Mary lectured her daughter about hanging up her clothes and making her bed before she left her room? Obviously it was a hard lesson for Abbott women to learn.

Hattie was alone in the kitchen, drinking a cup of coffee and reading the paper. She looked up as Susan came through the door, her impassive expression almost hiding her worry. "Still wearing those clothes, Miss Lou? I can't say as I blame you—this'll be your last chance. Mr. Marsden won't cotton to any wife of his wearing dungarees."

Susan shivered, not sure if it was the cool morning air or a presentiment of a bleak, frozen future. "He'll get used to it," she said firmly.

Hattie shook her head. "I don't think so, Miss

Lou. He's not the kind of man to make compromises.''

"Is he the kind of man to make me happy?"

"I think you already know the answer to that. You don't need me telling you what your heart has already told you a dozen times." She set the paper down, rising gracefully with her majestic bulk. "You want to take your coffee outside with you this morning?"

"Is there anyone lurking?"

Hattie chuckled. "Just Miss Mary, and I haven't seen her for a while. If I know Mr. Marsden you won't be seeing him until you get to the church. He's the kind of man to pay close attention to tradition."

"And my parents?"

"Still in bed. Sleeping off the effects of last night, I expect. Anyone else you're interested in?" The question was asked in an entirely bland tone of voice, but she wasn't fooled. Hattie was possibly the wisest person in this household.

"Jack," she said.

"Funny you should ask about him, Miss Lou. Mr. McGowan stopped by here no more than an hour ago, on his way to the early train to New York. He left a note for you." Hattie pulled a crisply folded piece of white paper out of her apron pocket.

She stared at it for a moment, reluctant to pluck it from Hattie's strong fingers. Her entire future, and that of her family, might depend on what was in that note. Did he tell Lou to marry Neddie and live happily ever after? Did he tell her he loved her, that he'd always loved her?

She took the paper and shoved it into her pocket with a nonchalant air. "I'll read it later," she said airily. "It's probably just good wishes on my upcoming marriage."

Hattie's snort was both inelegant and expressive. "I raised you smarter than that, Miss Lou." She turned back to the table, shrugging. "Let me know what you decide."

"I wasn't aware I had any decisions to make," Susan said.

"And when did you get into the habit of lying to me?" Hattie demanded.

Susan took her coffee and fled.

There was no sign of Mary anywhere about. The piece of paper was burning a hole in her pocket, but Hattie was watching her out of the kitchen window, and there was no way Susan would admit her curiosity. Particularly if she didn't like what the note had to say. She didn't want to cry in front of anyone.

Though heaven knows, if she were to cry in front of anyone it would be Hattie. She knew instinctively that Hattie was the best mother she had, full of comfort and common sense. She just wasn't sure she was ready to be mothered.

Speaking of which, she had to find her real mother. The preadolescent one, who was somewhere out in the sprawling, landscaped back gardens.

She called her name, not too loudly so as not to

wake the sleeping dragons upstairs, but there was no answer. She followed the path, her feet bare on the dew-damp grass, heading for the huge old maple tree at the edge of the forest, heading there instinctively. There was a marble bench beneath it, a place where Lou would sit for hours, reading, dreaming. She didn't wonder how she knew things like that—by now it had all become second nature to her.

She sat down, pulling the piece of paper out of her pocket and folding it open. It didn't say much.

"Lizzie B. 37th and 12th. 3:30 p.m., June 10th, 1949."

As a farewell letter it was a little too cryptic for her tastes. Who was Lizzie B., and what was he doing with her at three-thirty this afternoon, presumably in New York City?

Maybe he'd left the wrong note. Maybe this was a reminder for himself, and his terse farewell note was still stuck in his pocket. Or maybe it was a flowery note of farewell. And maybe pigs could fly.

She leaned back against the thick trunk of the maple, shutting her eyes as she crumpled the note in her hand. She took a deep, steadying breath, surprised to hear how ragged it sounded.

"You aren't going to marry him, are you?" Mary's voice floated down from the tree above her head.

It took all Susan's self-restraint not to jump. "He never asked me," she said, not bothering to disguise her mournful tone. "Not really."

Mary swung down out of the tree, landing in the dirt beside her. "I'm not talking about Jack," she said irritably. "I'm talking about Neddie. Don't do it for my sake, Lou. I know something's going on, I don't know what it is, but Elda and Father are up to something and it's probably something bad. Don't marry Neddie if you don't want to."

"Why wouldn't I want to? He's rich and handsome and he adores me."

"He's not as cute as Jack and we both know it, and he doesn't adore anyone but himself."

"He's still rich," she said wryly.

"And you've never cared one bit about money. Have they threatened you with something?"

Mary was smarter than any nine-year-old had a right to be. "I don't mind, Mary," she said, the name sounding both familiar and odd. "It's not like there's anyone else I want to marry, or would be likely to. If I marry Neddie then everyone will be taken care of."

"I don't want you to marry him."

"It's not as if I have any choice."

"Do you still think you're not the real Lou? Because if you're not, you must be here for a reason, and I'm willing to bet that reason wasn't to marry someone like Neddie Marsden."

"I don't know who I am anymore," she said, shoving the crumpled piece of paper back in her pocket. "It doesn't seem like I really have a choice." Jack was gone, leaving nothing more than a cryptic name, and she was hardly likely to go after a man who'd never said he loved her, and was already meeting another woman.

"You always have a choice. Haven't you and Hattie taught me that?" Mary said.

Susan looked up at the house. There were already signs of feverish activity. The mess from the rehearsal dinner had already been cleared away, but there were trucks pulling up the wide, winding driveway, more catering trucks, flower trucks. "I don't know, Mary," she said. "Do we always have a choice?" She could see Elda and Ridley advancing on her from the house, looking like the front guard of an invading army. They certainly weren't going to allow her to have any choice in the matter. If she didn't watch it they'd strip her, bathe and present her to Neddie on a silver platter in exchange for—

For what? Money? Power? Some kind of amnesty? If she knew exactly what kind of deal had been struck, maybe there'd be a way out of it. But she was running out of time.

"The hairdresser's already here!" Elda hissed in rage. "What in God's name are you doing out here, when there's so much to do? And in those clothes! I couldn't believe it when I saw you out here. Even Hattie had no idea where you'd disappeared to!"

Hattie had known exactly where she was, but she'd covered for her, bless her heart. "What do I have to do this morning?" Susan countered mildly enough. "I have to be dressed and made beautiful, transported to the church and say 'I do.' It doesn't sound too onerous.''

Elda's lip curled in disgust. She hadn't left the house without her makeup, but in her haste her orangey lipstick was slightly askew, giving her a faintly clownlike appearance. "As long as you cooperate there shouldn't be any problem. And you do intend to cooperate, don't you, Tallulah? You'll be a good, dutiful daughter.''

Susan looked at Ridley, wondering if he'd evince even a shred of guilt. He avoided her gaze, looking at Mary with a faint expression of displeasure. "You need to get changed, as well, missy,'' he said sternly. "You're a junior bridesmaid, and you haven't got your sister's physical blessings to help you. It's going to take more of an effort to turn you into a silk purse.''

Mary didn't even blink, for all the world as if she weren't an adolescent hovering on the brink of womanhood, easily shattered by a father's thoughtless words. "Don't worry, Father,'' she said in her cool, precocious voice. "I'm an Abbott. I'll rise to the occasion.''

Her faintly cynical tone swept right past him. "That's right,'' he said, not bothering to disguise his relief. "You're both Abbotts. Blood will tell, in the end. You both know your duty, and I expect you to do it with no shirking.''

"And what's your duty, Ridley?'' Susan came to him, towering over him. Her grandfather, her father, a small, selfish little man. Her mother never talked about him, but then, Mary's tenet had been to speak no evil. "Isn't it to support and protect your family? To be honorable and strong and just? Isn't that what a father's supposed to be?"

"How dare you speak to me like that?" Ridley fumed, white with rage. "After all I've done for you…"

"What? What have you done for me?"

"Given you everything you ever wanted. Money and clothes and new cars and a fancy house. I gave my family the good life, and I compromised myself to do it."

"Liar," she said softly. "You gave yourself the good life, and you don't care who pays for it and how."

For a moment she thought he would slap her. "I'm fifty-one years old, Tallulah. Too old to go to jail for any stupid mistakes I might have made, too old to start over again. Too old to be poor. You understand me? Neddie is willing to take you and keep things going as they have been, and I won't let you mess things up. You'll marry him, with a smile on your face, and you'll be the perfect little wife. You'll provide him a good home, you'll be the perfect hostess, and no one will even guess you ever had any second thoughts."

"And if I don't?"

All he had to do was glance at the stricken Mary, who listened to all this in horror. "You know who'll pay the most, don't you? Who has the most to lose. You'll do it.''

Elda came up to her and tucked her arm through Susan's, suddenly oozing charm. "This is just bridal nerves, Tallulah. I know we've had our differences, but you'll find this will all work out beautifully. After all, you were the one who wanted to marry Neddie. And you'll like being a married woman, having all that lovely money at your disposal. As long as you're discreet, do your job as wife and hostess, then you could be very happy."

The walls were closing in around her, and all avenues of escape seemed to be shut off. Where could she run to? She was a stranger in a strange time and place, with no one but herself to turn to. How could she protect Mary from the consequences of Ridley's selfish greed?

"Come along, dear," Elda said, tugging at her with only a trace of impatience, all spurious warmth and concern. "You don't want anyone to see you like this on your wedding day, and the photographers will be arriving soon. Mary, you go ahead and get ready, and I'll come in and help once the bridesmaids get here."

There was no choice, Susan had been right about that. They walked slowly back to the house, the four of them, the condemned prisoner, her confederate and the two jailers, Susan thought. For some reason the notion didn't amuse her. She'd lost her sense of humor somewhere along the way.

She went through the motions in a daze, bathing in the rose-scented water, sitting patiently while the hairdresser fussed and fiddled with her hair and makeup. The thick satin wedding dress slid over her body, and she closed her eyes, waiting for lightning to strike.

"You need a cigarette." Cousin Ginny, who'd left the baby behind this morning and was dressed in a peach bridesmaid's dress.

They set the veil on her head, a simple medieval-style headdress that matched the gown. "I don't know why you chose this," another bridesmaid muttered. "It's so plain!"

"It's elegant," Ginny said. "Different. Like Lou."

Susan looked at her reflection in the mirror. The tulle veil flowed down her back, her carefully arranged curls were tucked with flowers and lace. Her cheeks were rouged, her lips were crimson, her eyes were empty.

"You look gorgeous," Elda said briskly. "Come along, now. The limousines are here."

Susan rose. Or was she Tallulah? Walking to the door, to her fate, like an automaton, not sure she could fight anymore.

Mary was waiting for her, dressed in a ridiculously frilly dress chosen by some sadist.

She reached up and kissed Susan on her cheek. "Don't marry him," she whispered. "Promise me."

Susan drew back, looking down at Mary, and she

could see the future in her eyes. It was that simple. She had to change that future, that was why she was here.

She smiled, suddenly sure. "I promise," she said. And, lifting her heavy satin skirts, she followed Elda and her gaggle of bridesmaids out to the waiting limousines.

Chapter Fourteen

They arrived at the church at ten forty-five. The place was already packed—cars were parked along the side streets, and the double front doors of the church stood open to the June sunshine.

Susan had made the ride in silence, and if her chattering bridesmaids noticed, they probably put it down to a normal bride's need for reflection in the hour before her life changed forever.

They would have been half-right. She needed time for reflection, Susan thought, but she was about as far from a normal bride as anyone could imagine.

And her thought was simple—how the hell was she going to manage to stop this wedding?

Neddie had both threatened and ignored her when she'd tried to break the engagement. Elda and Ridley were waiting for her at the entrance to the church, both resplendent in their understated finery, and there was no way they'd let her get more than two feet in the wrong direction.

The silly bridesmaids were no help at all—they

piled out of the limousine ahead of her, shrieking with laughter, totally oblivious to the tension between the main players of this little drama.

Mary sat across from Susan, her thin young hands pressed against her bony knees beneath the frilly peach satin dress. "Don't do it, Lou," she said. "It's not too late."

Susan peered up the front steps of the church, pushing her veil back. "You think they're going to give me any chance to escape? I don't think so."

"You're the kind of woman who makes her own chances," Mary said. "And don't worry about me. I'm a survivor, like you. I don't care if we lose our money, our house, I don't care if Father goes to jail. He probably deserves it ten times over. Take your chance and run for it if you can, and don't look back."

"What if I can't come back? What if I never see you again?"

"Then I'll know I have the strongest, bravest sister in the world, someone who knew what was important, someone who went after what she wanted, went after the man she loved, and didn't take the safe, easy way out. If I ever have a daughter I'd want her to be just like you."

I am your daughter, Susan wanted to say, but clearly Mary chose to forget her temporary aberration. "Who says I'm in love?" she countered instead.

Ridley was advancing on the limousine, a determined expression on his faintly petulant face. Susan turned to the other side of the car, but there was no door there to provide her a last-minute escape.

"Don't lie to me, Lou, and don't lie to yourself," Mary said with precocious sternness. "You don't have any more time to waste."

Ridley reached into the car, took her arm and hauled her out with surprising strength for such a small man. "No more delays, my girl. All our friends are in there, waiting for you."

"I need to speak to Neddie," she said desperately, trying to pull free from his iron grip. Mary had scrambled out of the car behind her and was already racing up the wide stone steps of St. Anne's.

"You'll have a lifetime to speak to Neddie. There's nothing that can't wait."

She fought harder, fighting for her very life. "I can't—"

He slapped her full across the face, the force of the blow shocking her into stunned silence.

"No more, Tallulah!" He was pale and sweating with stress and fury. "You'll do your duty, and I don't want to hear another word about it." He began dragging her up the front steps of the church.

Her face burned with the imprint of his hand. She stumbled after him, numb, vaguely aware that there were no witnesses, only Mary standing by the entrance, watching with a stricken expression.

Ridley paused at the entrance of the church. The organ music drifted on toward "Oh Promise Me," and Susan jerked her head upward in delayed fury. Tallulah's father reached up and twitched the veil over her face.

"If anyone notices the mark on your face you can tell people you slipped," he hissed.

"If anyone notices, they'll just think Neddie did it," Susan said bitterly.

"Come along," Ridley snapped, shoving an immense, exotic bouquet in her numb, gloved hands. There were huge lilies, their scent overpowering, and she was reminded of death and funerals. He began to pull her into the shadowy church.

On cue the music switched to "Here Comes the Bride," and the entire congregation rose. Ridley began pulling the reluctant bride down the aisle.

Her feet seemed to have a mind of their own, instinctively moving in measured cadence to the sound of the wedding march. Neddie waited at the end of the aisle, a smug, portentous look on his ruddy face as he murmured something to his best man, and in front of her Mary stalled and dawdled as she dumped clumps of rose petals on the pale strip of carpet, Ridley's grip on her arm was painful, and the beaming approval of the packed church passed her in a blur.

She knew the drill, she'd suffered through the rehearsal the previous night, and she'd been to enough weddings. With Father Thomas looking like a benevolent elf, she would be handed from Ridley's manaclelike grip to Neddie's iron fist, and short of some dramatic declaration like "I don't!" she was well and truly trapped.

"Dearly beloved," Father Thomas intoned.

In the end it was simple. At the "who gives this woman?" part, Ridley followed his sexist cue and handed her over like a sack of flour, and Susan looked up into Neddie's florid face and simply, gracefully, collapsed in a spurious faint.

The shocked buzz of the congregation made it clear in this pretelevision generation that they hadn't seen brides and grooms collapse on "America's Funniest Home Videos."

"Give her some air," Neddie thundered, making no effort to touch her. She kept her eyes closed, hoping the heavy veiling would obscure the fact that she'd never felt healthier or more energetic in her life.

Mary knelt down beside her, plucking the bouquet from her limps hands and tossing it to one side. She leaned over to lift the veil, her face white with panic, and Susan muttered beneath her breath, "Leave it."

A moment later she was jerked to her feet, but she had the presence of mind to go limp against her fiancé, drooping affectingly. "She'll be fine in a moment," he announced in a loud voice that barely concealed his fury. "We'll just get her some fresh air and then continue with the wedding."

Mary was at her other side, helping her, and Susan gave her hand a reassuring squeeze as they made their slow way back down the aisle, tramping over the scattered rose petals. She had the sudden absurd thought that they ought to be playing the wedding march backward as they retraced their steps, and she had to stifle a semihysterical giggle as they came out into the bright, clear sunshine.

Neddie made the dire mistake of releasing her, shoving her away from him in petulant fury, but Mary still held on. A moment later Susan felt something hard and metallic pressed into her hand, and instinctively she knew what it was. Car keys. Car keys with a rabbit's foot key ring, the kind that Todd Abbott had. And Todd's convertible was parked across the street, waiting.

"What kind of game are you playing, Tallulah? I won't be made a fool of."

"You already are a fool, Neddie," Mary said with devastating frankness, releasing Susan and confronting the ogre with unflinching courage. "She's not going to marry you."

"I'll ruin your family. Your father will end up in jail...."

"If you have any sense at all you'll come up with a believable excuse, if you don't want to be the butt of jokes for the rest of your life," Susan said, ripping the veil off her head and tossing it on the stone steps. The satin sleeves of her dress were too long, and she shoved them up to her elbows, ready to do battle. "And if you hurt my sister I'll make you pay."

"Oh, I'm terrified," Neddie said with a smirk.

It was the last straw. She came up to him, eye to

eye, poking him in the chest. "You should be, Neddie. I know things you couldn't even begin to guess. I can see the future, and I have powers that would astonish you. And I have awful ways of taking revenge."

"So you're a witch, are you? It's going to take more than that to convince me."

"How about this?" The shoes were good for more than kicking Jack McGowan in the shins. They were also excellent for treading on the instep of unwanted fiancés. He let out a shriek of pain, she shoved him against the stone edifice, blew a kiss to Mary and took off, racing down the wide front steps, her wedding gown caught in her hands.

She didn't bother with the door to Todd's car, she simply leaped over the side. She didn't waste time looking back to see whether Neddie was following her, she simply let out the clutch, ground the gears, and took off into the bright morning sunshine, tearing down the road.

It was after two o'clock by the time she reached New York. On the one hand traffic was astonishingly nonexistent—on a Saturday in 1949 there were no commuters, and the comparatively few vehicles on a Merritt Parkway that had obviously never heard of road rage.

On the other hand, the roads were narrow, windy, two-way and slow. And Todd's car, for all its hot-rod appeal, couldn't make it much past fifty-five.

She had absolutely no idea what she'd find at 37th

and 12th. It might not even be an address. She could only hope she'd find Jack. What she'd say to him was another matter entirely, something she was leaving up to fate. She had taken it on faith that she needed to follow him. Somehow, sometime Susan Abbott had ceased to exist. She still remembered her own past, or was it the future. She still didn't recognize or know Tallulah's life.

But her heart and soul had become Lou. She was in love with Jack McGowan, and all she knew was she had to tell him.

He was meeting the mysterious Lizzie B. down by the docks. She should have realized that address would be on the Hudson River. She could see the ocean liners, the tramp steamers, the cargo ships lined up for what seemed like miles. She parked the car on the corner of 37th Street, scarcely wondering at the miracle of finding a parking spot in Manhattan with no trouble. She doubted life was idyllic enough to keep the roadster from being stolen, but that in itself might save her cousin's life. Maybe if Todd didn't own a car, he wouldn't go off that bridge and die.

She climbed out of the car, her long skirts in her hands, and started towards the corner. She had no purse, no identification, no money, no clothes but the satin wedding dress, which was hardly appropriate dockside apparel. She didn't care. She had put herself in the hands of fate, willing to take chances. She was

Lou now, and Lou was brave and adventurous. Careful Susan Abbott was long gone.

There was no sign of anyone. It was almost three-thirty, the time of the appointed meeting, and the only people she saw were the crew of the steamer busily getting ready for departure. She looked up at it for a moment, curious. It was big, sturdy, a little raffish. Just like Jack McGowan.

And then she looked at the name of the ship, knowing what she'd find. The *Lizzie B.*

No one stopped her as she made her way up the gangplank, though she garnered a few strange looks in her wedding finery. They were all too busy getting ready to leave. She finally collared a busy young sailor on the deck.

"I'm looking for Jack McGowan."

He did a double take, then grinned. "I can show you his cabin, but I don't know where he is at the moment. What did he do, leave you at the altar?"

"No one leaves me anywhere," she said in a mock stern voice. "I'm his going-away present."

"I'm sure he'll appreciate it," the young man said. "And are you a surprise?"

"Mmm-hmm. If you see him before we sail, don't tell him I'm here."

"You got it."

She followed him into the shadowy companionway, down two flights of metal stairs, her long skirts dragging. His cabin was small, with a porthole overlooking the river and a single narrow bunk. Room enough, she decided cheerfully.

"Good luck," the young man said cheerfully. "I'm Cafferty, by the way. Second mate. I expect I'll be seeing you on the trip."

"Unless he decides to throw me overboard." She kicked off her shoes and climbed onto the bunk.

"I doubt it. He just might not feel like leaving the cabin once he sees you. I know I wouldn't."

She grinned at him. He seemed very young and charmingly innocent. "You're very sweet. Let's just hope McGowan feels the same way."

"He will."

He shut the door behind him, and she leaned back against the bulkhead. The mattress was decently padded, though she was going to need another pillow at least. She closed her eyes, listening to the sound of the crew rushing about, the rumble of the engines beneath her. She was still wearing the delicate gold watch, and she slipped it off, along with the ugly diamond ring. They were engagement presents from Neddie, and she wanted nothing more to do with him, ever. She opened the porthole and tossed them into the Hudson River.

Lizzie B. began moving promptly at three-thirty. Susan sat and watched as they moved past the old buildings, quelling her initial nervousness at unbidden memories of a few too many viewings of *Titanic*. Lou Abbott didn't marry Neddie Marsden, and she didn't die in a train wreck. She certainly wasn't about to die in a shipwreck, either. Her future spread out before her, full of limitless possibilities.

She dozed off for a while, waiting for him. The fresh flowers in her hair wilted, the petals falling beneath her, and her thick mass of hair came loose. It was late, almost dark when the door of the cabin opened, and they'd been out at sea for hours.

For a moment he didn't see her. She lay very still on the bunk, watching him, and he looked weary, angry, depressed. He'd shed his coat and tie, his shirt was rumpled, he needed a shave, and he was the most gorgeous thing she'd ever seen in her life. She wondered if there was any way she could convince him never to wear a suit again in his life.

And then he saw her. He froze, just inside the open cabin door, staring at her in disbelief.

"Surprise," she said weakly. The moment of reckoning was at hand, and she was suddenly terrified. She didn't want to spend the rest of her life without the right man.

He closed the door behind him, locked it. That was a good sign. And then he came toward her, his expression unreadable. It was dusk in the cabin, but he hadn't bothered to turn on any lights, and he looked wary, hopeful. She saw that faint glimmer of hope in his dark eyes, and she knew with sudden certainty that everything would be all right.

"You want to tell me what happened?" he asked in his low, measured voice.

"I left Neddie at the altar. You could have been

a little more specific in that note you left. I thought *Lizzie B.* was another woman."

He didn't say anything for a moment. Then he spoke. "Why?"

Here was the hard part. The chance to be shot down, rejected, shamed. She drew her knees up beneath the satin gown and looked at him pensively. "Because I'm in love with you. I have been since I was twelve years old, and everybody knew it, including Jimmy."

"Don't you think it's time you grew up?"

"I did. I loved Jimmy—he was everything good and kind and decent. He was my best friend, and we would have been very happy together. But sometimes life doesn't work that way. Since I can't have a man who was good to me, good for me, then I might as well settle for you. Considering that I never got over you completely."

She managed to get him to smile at that. "You think I'm bad for you."

"And bad to me. But I expect a lot of that is just your natural curmudgeonly personality. The love of a good woman should mellow you."

"And you're that good woman?"

"No other. Don't even think about it. You see, you've missed an essential point in all this."

"And what's that?"

"You're in love with me. You feel guilty because of Jimmy, you think you're robbing the cradle, you think you don't have the right to be happy. And I think you're full of crap. If you thought about it, you'd know that nothing would make Jimmy happier than if we got married. And he'd be mad as hell if you dumped me.''

"You're probably right," he said lazily. "I didn't know you were proposing. I thought you were my bon voyage present.''

"You're not going anywhere without me. I'm yours, buster. And you're mine." She held her breath, waiting. She'd given it her best shot. They weren't too far out to sea that he couldn't manage to send her back if he were really determined. He loved her; she knew it. She just wasn't sure if he did.

"You're a formidable woman, Lou Abbott," he said finally.

"Yes."

"I guess I don't have much choice."

It wasn't exactly the declaration she was longing to hear. "Meaning?" she prompted, ready to throw something at him if he continued being obtuse.

"Meaning I can't risk disappointing my little brother. Meaning I'm not as stupid as I sometimes act."

He had long, beautiful hands, and he slid them through her hair, cupping her face, drawing it up to his. "Meaning I'm in love with you, which you've probably known longer than I have, and since you were kind enough to point it out to me, I'm not going to let you go."

She could feel her face crumple into a smile of such blazing magnitude that it shook her to her soul. He put his mouth against hers, she slid her arms around his neck, and a second later she was gone.

Part Three—Susan Returns

Chapter Fifteen

The mattress beneath her was hard, much harder than the bed in Tallulah's bedroom in Matchfield. She lay very still, the world whirling around her. She must be seasick. The pitch and roll of the bunk beneath her was powerful, and she gripped the sheet beneath her for some kind of ballast.

At least the cabin didn't smell like cigarette smoke—that would have been the final straw to her churning stomach. For the first time in days she couldn't smell stale smoke.

He was sitting by the window, as he had been when she first woke up, and she wondered what he'd do if she suddenly threw up. You could tell a real hero if he didn't flinch from a woman becoming violently ill.

"You need me to get a bucket and hold your head?" His voice was odd in the darkness, both tender and amused, and Susan took a deep breath, trying to still her roiling stomach. It came as no surprise. She already knew she loved this man desperately.

"Jack?" she murmured, her voice odd, lighter, breathier.

The bunk beneath her stopped pitching. It was wider than a bunk, wider than the twin bed in Lou's bedroom. She felt him cross the room, standing over her, and she was suddenly afraid to open her eyes.

"Jake," he corrected her. "Jake Wyczynski, remember?"

Her eyes flew open. "Oh, my God," she croaked.

His grin was crooked. "No, Jake Wyczynski," he corrected her again. "How are you feeling? You've been dead to the world—Mary was wondering whether she was going to have to call off the wedding. Frankly, I think she would have been more than happy to do so."

She looked up at him, dizzy and disoriented. It had been a dream. Of course it had—she'd known it all along, even while she was in the midst of it. Maybe.

"Where is my mother?" Her voice still felt strange to her, light and cool, not warm and husky.

"Alex convinced her to go out for dinner, and I promised I'd sit with you. It's a good thing you decided to finally wake up—she was going to call the paramedics if you hadn't surfaced by tonight."

"Who's Alex? And what day is it?"

Jake didn't even blink, but Susan wasn't so confused that she didn't recognize the faint shifting expression. "It's Friday night, kiddo. You're marrying your true love at four o'clock tomorrow afternoon."

She pushed herself up in the bed, shaking her head slightly to clear it. No long dark tresses swinging around her face, and without thinking she grabbed her chest. Thirty-four-A once more. Damn.

Of course Jake didn't miss a thing. "I didn't touch you," he drawled. "I like my woman awake and willing."

She looked up at him. He towered over the bed, a tall man with a lean, rangy body. His hair was far too long, pushed back from his deeply tanned face, and lines fanned out around his light blue eyes. He was wearing old jeans and a khaki shirt, and for the first time she realized he was wearing a small gold hoop in one ear. He looked like a pirate. He looked like Jack McGowan.

He looked like the man she loved.

She was still out of her mind, she decided briskly, throwing back the covers. "What about the wedding rehearsal? The rehearsal dinner?"

"You didn't want a rehearsal dinner, remember? You said there was too much stuff going on this week already, and you wanted the night before the wedding to be peaceful. And your mother stood in for you during the rehearsal. She said you were tired and needed your rest. Obviously, since you've been asleep since Wednesday afternoon."

"Obviously." She looked down at her familiar/ unfamiliar body. She was wearing an oversize cotton

T-shirt and panties, and she supposed she should find a bathrobe or something or wrap the sheet around her, but she couldn't bring herself to bother. Jake was a grown-up—he would hardly be overcome with lust.

"I need coffee," she said. "Good coffee that doesn't come in a can."

"Hey, I can arrange that. You take a shower and get dressed, and it'll be waiting for you."

Her head was pounding. She reached up to thread her fingers through her hair, shocked at the thick, close-cropped length of it. And then she looked up at Jake. "You still didn't tell me who Alex is."

There was only the faintest softening in Jake's cynical expression. "I think you can guess, Susan. He's your father. He came back for your wedding."

The day had definitely gone from bad to worse, Susan thought, standing under the shower as she tried to wash the fog from her mind. Her small breasts felt unfamiliar beneath her soapy hands, her skin felt odd, prickly, and for the first time she didn't feel cold. She felt hot, edgy, confused.

Somewhere she'd managed to lose three days, and now she was back, just as if nothing had ever happened. Back with Jake Wyczynski, a man almost as unsettling as the dreams that had plagued her.

Or was it a dream? Had she slept for days, or had she really traveled back in time, into her Aunt Tallulah's body? There was only one way to tell. If it were true, then she'd manage to change history. Aunt Tallulah hadn't died in a train wreck on her way to her honeymoon, she hadn't married Ned Marsden. She'd run off with the man she'd always loved, and maybe she was still alive somewhere, having the time of her life.

It felt good to wear a thin wisp of a lace bra again, good to slip into baggy jeans and an oversize T-shirt. By the time she wandered out into her mother's kitchen, the smell of French Roast coffee was strong in the air.

He handed her a mug without speaking, and it was just the way she liked it, black and strong and sweet. She didn't bother asking him how he knew she took her coffee with sugar only. There were other, far more important questions plaguing her.

"Your mother's waiting for you in the living room," he said. "And I think I'll make myself scarce. I've got to figure out what I'm going to wear for your wedding. Assuming it's still on?" There was a faint question in his voice.

"It's still on," she said grimly, wondering if she was out of her mind. "I can't imagine why you'd want to come."

"You've said that before. I'm ignoring you. I promised Louisa I'd come, and I keep my promises."

"I thought I told you the last time I saw you that I didn't want you coming to the wedding?"

"Funny you should mention the last time you saw me. I don't remember that we did much talking."

She could still taste him. His mouth against hers,

slow, deliberate, a kiss that could destroy a lifetime of well-laid plans.

"Really?" she said in a light voice. "I'd forgotten."

He didn't say a word, his expression of disbelief was enough. "Don't waste your time, kid. Go talk to your mother. She wants to see for certain you're all right."

"Is she alone?"

"Yup. She sent Alex away when I told her you were up. You gonna give her a hard time?"

Susan took a deep breath. Four days ago the answer would have been an unequivocal yes. Now life was no longer the certainty she'd counted on. Mary Abbott had been her best friend, her confidante, her savior. Both in this life and in the past. "That's my business, don't you think?"

He shrugged. "You've got some wedding presents from your godmother to catch up on. I'll see you tomorrow."

She didn't want him to leave. Standing in the kitchen, barefoot, defiant, she didn't want him to leave her. She wasn't ready to face her mother. She wasn't ready to face her life. Instead she wanted to throw everything away and run off with him. Crazy, because she'd worked so hard to get what she wanted, and Jake was just the kind of man she'd always avoided.

"Sure," she said carelessly. "I'll be the one in white."

"Will I get to kiss the bride?" It seemed like a smart-ass, casual question, and maybe Susan only imagined the thread of tension beneath the light tone.

"You already did," she said.

"I could do it again."

She looked up at him, startled. She wanted him to. Desperately. She moved, almost imperceptibly, and he reached out his hand, almost touching her, when Mary appeared in the kitchen doorway.

"Susan?" she said in her soft voice. "I've been so worried about you, sweetie." She swept her into a deliciously scented embrace, smelling of her classic Chanel. The last time she'd hugged Mary she'd smelled of chocolate.

"I'm fine, Mother," she said, pulling away just a little to look down into her mother's eyes. The same warm brown ones, but far wiser than they had been at age nine. "I was just very tired."

"I'd say that was an understatement," Jake drawled, back in his corner of the kitchen.

Mary was looking up at her with an odd expression on her face. "Go away, Jake," Susan said. "I need to talk with my mother privately. After all, I am getting married tomorrow."

"Honey, if you don't know the facts of life yet I'll be more than happy to save your mother the trouble of explaining them to you."

"You're annoying, you know that?" Susan said severely.

"I try to be."

"You succeed beyond your wildest dreams."

"Susan!" Her mother admonished her. "Why in the world are you treating Jake like that? He's been absolutely wonderful, running errands, calming my fears, sitting by your bed for hours on end. I don't know what I would have done without him. I can't even begin to tell Louisa how grateful I am, and you should be grateful, as well."

Jake grinned, pushing away from the kitchen counter. He didn't touch her as he passed her. He didn't need to. For some reason his very presence, the heat from his body, was palpable. "I don't know how grateful your daughter is."

She wanted to kick him, but she didn't have the right shoes on. And she'd already done it.

No, that was Tallulah. Lou had kicked Jack McGowan, a perfectly reasonable move since she was madly in love with him. Whereas Susan had no logical reason to kick Jake Wyczynski. Apart from the fact that he was terminally infuriating.

"She'll express her thanks later," Mary said, shooing him out of the house with such perfect manners that most men wouldn't even realize they'd been dismissed. Jake wasn't most men, however, and he didn't miss much.

Susan took her coffee and wandered back into the living room, looking at it with fresh eyes. She recognized the secretary desk in the corner—it had been in Tallulah's bedroom. So had the china dogs on the mantel. She was holding one when her mother came back into the room.

She set the porcelain figurine back on the mantel and turned to her mother. There was only one way to find out whether she'd dreamed it all. "Will Aunt Tallulah be coming to the wedding?"

It was a stupid way to phrase it, and for a moment Mary Abbott looked truly shocked. And then she sat on the toile-covered sofa, small and graceful, not much bigger than she had been at age nine, and looked up at her daughter. "You know perfectly well my sister died on her wedding day in 1949, Susan," she said. "She's hardly going to rise from the grave at this late date. If that's your idea of a joke then I must say it's in extremely bad taste."

"I'm sorry," Susan muttered, guilt and disorientation warring with the tangled memories. "It's just that I had the strangest dreams while I was asleep, and they seemed so real."

"Did you? What did you dream?"

"That I traveled back fifty years and saved Lou's life."

Mary's odd expression was tinged with sorrow. "You can't change the past, Susan. You can only change the future. As a matter of fact, I had strange dreams about my sister as well, and I haven't dreamed about her in years."

"I'm sorry I couldn't save her for you."

"I'm sorry you couldn't, too, sweetie. But I'm very happy to have you back among the living, wide-awake. There's something I want to talk to you about. Your father's back.''

"I know. I saw him before I fell asleep."

"And?"

Her mother was utterly patient, seemingly focused on her daughter's reaction. She would send him away if Susan told her to, send him away without hesitation. And part of Susan wanted nothing more than to banish the man who'd abandoned them.

But if she'd learned one thing from the past few days, she'd learned that things weren't always as they seemed. And if Alex had married little Mary Abbott, daughter of Ridley and Elda, then the odds would have been stacked against him in the first place.

"Why did he come back? Does he think he's going to give me away? He never had me in the first place, did he?"

"No, he didn't," Mary said patiently. "He left, and nothing will change that. Shall I tell him to go away?"

"Do you want to?" Susan already knew the answer. The answer to questions that had plagued her all her life. She still didn't know why or how her parents had parted, but she knew why her mother had never remarried. She was still in love with her husband.

Her mother still hadn't said anything. In the fifty years since she'd last seen her, Mary Abbott had become a master of diplomacy and caution, a far cry from the passionate girl who'd lost her older sister.

Susan gave herself a little shake. Hadn't she already proven that it was nothing more than a crazy dream? "Invite him to the wedding," she said finally. "He can sit with you."

"I already did."

She hadn't changed that much in fifty years. There was still a streak of stubborn mischief beneath the calm exterior. "I know," Susan said.

"I should call Edward and tell him you're awake," Mary said, and there was only the hint of a question in her voice.

"I suppose you managed to send him into a panic, as well. I was just tired, mother."

"That's what Edward said. He had no doubt that you simply needed a good long rest and you'd wake up in plenty of time for the wedding. He seemed slightly annoyed that you had to miss the rehearsal and two of the dinner parties planned in your honor, but he carried on without you, once I assured him you looked quite healthy."

"He didn't check for himself?"

"No, dear. I suspect Edward is like most men— absolutely useless around any kind of illness. He reminds me a bit of my father."

"That's an awful thing to say!" Susan protested hotly.

Mary looked at her strangely. "Your grandfather

died when you were three years old, Susan. You'd hardly remember him."

There was no way Susan could explain her sudden revulsion. In truth, Ridley Abbott could have been a charming, devoted father. Mary had certainly never said otherwise. And she'd never voiced a single criticism of Elda. Or mentioned that Elda was her stepmother rather than her real mother.

It was all a dream, Susan told herself. None of it happened, none of it was real. Tallulah died in a train wreck on her wedding day, Ridley and Elda were devoted parents, and Mary had no secrets.

"Do I look like Elda?" she demanded abruptly. There were only a few family pictures at the Abbott house, and none of Ridley's wife. The Elda Susan had dreamed about was small, dark, brittle and sophisticated. The antithesis of Susan.

"Not likely," Mary said. "Elda was my father's second wife. My stepmother. There'd be no reason for you to resemble her."

Susan felt suddenly chilled. "You never told me that."

"Didn't I?" Mary said vaguely. "I would have thought I'd mentioned it. And no, you don't look like her at all."

"What did she look like?"

"Elda died over twenty years ago, Susan. Why would you care?"

"Humor me. She was in my dreams."

"Then you know what she looked like."

"Mother!"

Mary sighed. "She looked a little like Joan Crawford, actually. She was dark and tiny and very polished. And she always wore orange lipstick. Odd, I almost forgot about that."

Susan could see her so clearly it shook her—Elda's thin, chilly smile, painted in orange.

"I'm going out," she said abruptly.

"You can't! It's after ten o'clock."

"I need to...to talk with someone." She had no idea who she could turn to, she only knew she had to get away from her mother.

"Susan, you're getting married at four o'clock tomorrow afternoon. Unless you've changed your mind?"

"Why do people keep asking me that?" she demanded. "Why shouldn't I marry Neddie?"

Mary turn pale. "Edward," she corrected her in a shocked voice. "You're going to marry Edward."

"Maybe," she said. Thinking of Neddie Marsden and Jack and Jake, the two of them so different and yet so alike. Maybe, she thought.

Maybe.

Chapter Sixteen

Jake Wyczynski was in a foul mood. One of the worst he could ever remember. He kept trying to think back to some time in his thirty-five years when he'd felt this cantankerous. There was the time in Singapore, when he and his uncle Jack had gone drinking at some waterfront dive. Uncle Jack had had one of his rare fights with Louisa, and Jake had felt like raising a little hell.

A broken hand and seventeen stitches later, he'd felt a little more mellow, and Uncle Jack had been inordinately proud of himself. There weren't many seventy-two-year-olds who could still hold their own in a barroom brawl.

And then there was the time in Kenya, when Jake had run afoul of a local official and barely escaped with his skin intact. His uncle hadn't been with him that time, though he'd bemoaned that fact later.

But now Uncle Jack was dead, and Jake was still getting into trouble. It had been years since he'd gotten himself into such a mess—Aunt Louisa used to tell him he was getting positively staid. All he needed was a wife to make him as conservative as a banker.

He'd laughed at her, of course. She was just needling him—there was no way he'd ever settle down, not completely. And he certainly didn't need anything as ordinary as a wife. Not the same woman, day after day, year after year, through good times and bad. Not unless she was someone like Louisa.

But that was before he'd met Susan Abbott.

Funny, but she reminded him of a younger Louisa, and he wasn't quite sure why. They were both tall, though Louisa was stooped with age. They had different eye color, but there was something similar in their expression. A sort of a vulnerable, to-hell-with-you bravado that was both infuriating and enchanting. He'd spent half his life with his uncle Jack and aunt Louisa, and now he'd fallen for her clone.

No, she wasn't a clone. It would be easier to ignore her if she was. He'd always had a kind of crush on the magnificent Louisa—what young kid wouldn't have, and finding a youthful version of her was tempting. And he was so damned tempted he was going nuts.

The doors on the old garage were ridiculous—giant French doors with filthy glass. He shoved them open, letting the air rush into the place. It was late, the heat of the day had faded, and the wind was picking up, riffling through the trees. It felt more like home now—his tumbledown house in Spain, or the ruined palazzo in Venice. He wanted to be home now. But somehow the thought of it seemed empty.

Hell, he thought in total disgust, he was lying to himself, when he'd always made a practice of being scrupulously honest. He didn't want to go back to Spain, to that house, without Susan Abbott along to drive him crazy.

He shoved his wet hair back from his face. He'd gone swimming on his way back to the old garage—there was a pond hidden deep in the woods that was clear and cool, but it hadn't managed to chill his blood. Keeping watch over Susan while she slept, watching the rise and fall of her small, perfect breasts, the flicker of her eyelids as she dreamed, the softness of her lips, had driven him half-crazy with desire.

Maybe once he was out of here he'd forget about her. If he had any sense he'd skip the wedding and head on out tomorrow morning, and to hell with his promises to Louisa. It would be a simple matter to book passage on a tramp steamer and make his excuses later. Louisa would understand.

Or would she? He'd never been a coward in his entire life. Not a physical coward, not an emotional one. Why the hell was he starting now?

There was a sudden gust of wind, and he looked up. And froze. Susan Abbott was standing just inside the open door, and for a moment he had the strangest vision. She looked different, with long, flowing clothes and a mane of dark hair.

And then he blinked, and she was still standing there. In the jeans and T-shirt he'd last seen her in, looking as lost and confused as he felt.

He didn't move, afraid to make the wrong one. He was wearing nothing but an old pair of cutoffs that he'd pulled on after his swim, and maybe he should find a shirt, or maybe he shouldn't, if he was just going to take it off again. He watched her.

There was no electrical power in the old, abandoned building, and the place was only lit by a couple of oil lamps. It didn't matter. He could see her quite clearly, see the doubt and frustration in her eyes.

"I don't know why I'm here," she said.

"Don't you?" He kept his voice even, noncommittal. He felt like a horny teenager, acutely aware of the rumpled bed behind him. Wondering if she was thinking of it, too.

"I went to see Edward. To talk with him. But he was…preoccupied. Busy. I could see him through the window. So I ran away."

"With another woman?" he asked, trying to hide his surge of triumph.

Susan shook her head. "Worse. He was watching golf on TV."

Being a man, Jake couldn't quite see the criminality of such an act. "What's wrong with watching golf?"

"On the night before your wedding? When your

fiancée has decided to take a two-day siesta? It's a little cold-blooded, don't you think?''

"Edward never struck me as a particularly passionate sort," he offered.

"Neither am I." There was delicious doubt in her voice.

"I think you're wrong about that," he said. "You just haven't found the right man."

She managed to summon up the ghost of her old defenses. "And that would be you?" she said, faintly caustic.

"That would be me." The words astonished him with their rightness. For all his frustration and denial it was suddenly very clear. He was the right man. And she was the right woman.

"Do you play golf?" she asked suspiciously.

"Occasionally. But I never wear funny pants. And I never watch golf on TV. And you can be damned sure I wouldn't be spending my time alone when I could be with a woman like you."

He wondered who was going to make the first move. If he took a step toward her would she run away again? He didn't think he could stand it if she did.

"I can't marry Edward," she said in an odd voice.

He nodded, for lack of anything better to do. "Did you just figure that out?"

She shook her head. "I think I've known it for fifty years."

It made no sense, but then, it didn't need to. Again

her image wavered and shifted in the lamplight. And he gave up being patient.

He crossed the garage floor, but she held her ground, not running. When he reached her she looked up at him, her green eyes wary. Waiting.

"Are you afraid of me?"

"I suppose I'm afraid you'll abandon me," she said carefully. "People do. They leave all the time, and the only way to protect yourself is never to care in the first place. I don't think I could stand it if I were abandoned one more time. By someone who mattered."

"It doesn't work," he said grimly. "You can't stop feeling."

"You're right," she said. "And besides, it's too late. I already care."

"You're going to marry me," he said. He had no idea where those words had come from, he only knew they were right.

"Yes," she said, utterly without hesitation.

He slid his fingers through her short-cropped hair, tilting her face up to his. And then he kissed her, taking his time—a slow, languorous touch of mouth against mouth, tongue against tongue, building in increments of heat and desire until he found she was trembling and he was, too.

He didn't ask. He simply pulled her up tight against his body and took her to the bed. And she let him.

She was passive, almost childlike as he stripped

the clothes from her. She said nothing when he tossed her T-shirt and bra across the room, nothing when he shoved her jeans and underwear down her slender hips so she could step out of them. Nothing when he put his hands on her waist and drew her toward him. Nothing until he slid his hand between her legs, through her tangle of hair, and touched her.

She made a soft, gulping noise, and her hands came up to clutch his shoulders, tightly. He pushed her back on the bed, following her down, and she closed her eyes, averting her face as he touched her.

He let her get away with it. She was tight, barely damp, but he slid his fingers inside her, bringing her to orgasm with calm, almost mechanical efficiency. In one moment she was lying beside him, shutting him out, in the next she had arched off the bed with a strangled cry of shock.

He knew how to prolong it, almost past endurance, testing the waves of reaction that shuddered through her body, teasing and pushing at just the right moment to set off a new convulsion.

"Stop!" she whispered in a choked voice. "Please. Wait." He froze, but she continued to climax, her body out of control, waves of release racking her body until they finally subsided, leaving her limp, almost fragile looking in the tumbled bed.

He was more than ready to explode himself, but she looked so worn-out that he didn't touch her. He simply sat back, watching her, his body iron hard with tension and desire.

He could control it, he told himself, taking a deep, shuddering breath. He could give her time, even if it killed him, he could wait until she was ready for more, even if it took all night....

Her face was wet with tears, but guilt had no effect on him. He sat there, frozen, when she suddenly opened her eyes.

"Whew!" she said in a weak voice. And then, to his amazement, a soft, lascivious smile curved her mouth. "I needed that." And she reached for the waistband of his cutoffs, tugging him toward her as she slipped her hand inside to touch him.

He didn't remember how he managed to strip his pants off, but he did so in record time. He was blind with need, wild with it, wild with wanting her, and the calm, sane part of him had vanished into some dark, dangerous place, where all that mattered was Susan, reaching for him, opening for him, taking him deep inside her as she wrapped her body around his and held him tight.

She kissed his mouth and stilled him. She touched his face and calmed him. She arched her back, taking him deep, deep inside, meeting his thrusts until he felt her shiver and clench around him, and he let go, tumbling down and down into the hot, wet darkness of soul-shattering completion.

He could feel the breeze blowing on his sweat-soaked back. He could sense the flickering oil lamps around them, and when he lifted his head to look at her, to say something, anything, declare his undying love, he saw that she was asleep. Again, as she had been for the past two days.

He climbed off her, carefully, but she was dead to the world. He lay beside her, pulling her up against his body, and she slept on, a faint, blissful smile on her face. He wrapped his arms around her, buried his face in her thick honey-colored hair and slept.

THERE WERE DREAMS. Vivid, sexual dreams. The bed rocked beneath them, and she didn't know whether it was from the power of their lovemaking or the roll of the ocean beneath their bunk. She didn't know whether she was Susan or Tallulah, she didn't know whether she lay with Jack or Jake.

It didn't matter. It was dark and gloriously sinful and utterly right, and she moved in the darkness, the breeze cooling her fevered skin as she slid over his body and took him deep within her, rocking and surging until she shattered around him, helpless in her powerful response, and he turned her beneath him and finished it. She hid her face against his chest, licking his skin, whispering dark and wicked secrets, and he kissed her eyelids and her throat, kissed the small of her back and behind her knees, and nothing mattered but that the night would never end.

But it did. And when Susan awoke in the rumpled bed in the ramshackle garage she was alone. Abandoned, as she'd always been afraid she would be.

She didn't bother to look for a note—she knew there wouldn't be one. Her body ached, she had scratch marks and bite marks and bruises that would make a hooker blush. She dressed herself, stealing one of his worn khaki shirts to add a little warmth to the morning chill. And she headed out along the path, refusing to look back.

Her car wouldn't start. There was no way in hell she'd go back to the garage, she simply started running, a slow, easy pace that got faster and faster, as she ran from her fears in the early sunrise hours.

Her mother's house was empty. It was six o'clock in the morning and her mother's bed hadn't been slept in, and Susan knew Mary had spent the night with the man she'd always loved. The wrong man, or the right man, who could know for sure?

It didn't matter. Susan had made the same mistake. Like mother, like daughter, like aunt. Throwing away a life for the sake of crazy passion. Throwing away comfort and security for uncertainty. She was as crazy as they were.

She took a long shower, wiping all trace of the night from her body. She called Edward, but his answering machine was on, and she had no idea where he'd be at that hour. She made some toast and ended up throwing it in the trash. And then she went back into her bedroom.

The wedding dress hung from a special hook over the door, the flowing satin gleaming in the early light. It didn't look as if she'd slept in it, it didn't look as if she'd traveled backward in time in it.

And for what reason? She hadn't been able to save

Tallulah, she hadn't been able to change a thing. She'd only complicated her own life past bearing.

Maybe she could go back again. Maybe if she put on the dress she'd be magically transported fifty years into the past, where life was simpler, and there weren't so many choices.

But that was bull. Life was just as complicated back then, and her mother had already told her the truth. You can't change the past, you can only change the future.

She stripped off her clothes and put on the wedding dress, staring at her reflection in the mirror, squinting, trying to see Tallulah looking back. But it wasn't her long-dead aunt, and it wasn't the familiar Susan, either. The woman in the mirror was different. Softer, sadder, more human. She looked vulnerable, Susan thought. Like a woman in love.

She blinked again, but the mirror didn't waver. Outside she heard a car drive into the driveway, but she didn't move. She'd lost the will to do anything but stand there, staring.

"You look gorgeous, darling." Edward's voice was like a glass of ice water thrown in her face. She whirled around, feeling her face turn pale with shock and then red with shame.

"I didn't hear you come in! Edward, you shouldn't be here..."

"Don't be silly, Susan. I don't believe in any superstitious garbage about not seeing the bride before the ceremony. We make our own luck. And I must say that's a spectacular dress. Mother's livid about her dress, of course, but I've managed to calm her down. Looking at you now, I'm glad her dress ripped.''

Susan stared at him numbly. "Edward..."

"Yes, love?"

"I can't marry you."

His Teflon smile faded slightly, and his perfect brow wrinkled slightly. "Bridal nerves, darling? I'm sure they'll pass."

She'd almost forgotten how impervious Edward was to subtleties. "I don't love you, Edward."

"I know that," he said with an expansive smile. "I don't love you, either. But we'll make a marvelous pair. We're perfectly suited to each other—haven't I always told you that?"

He had, indeed. He'd even managed to convince her of it for long enough to get her into this mess.

"You don't understand. I spent last night with someone else. In bed with someone else. Making love with someone else."

His smile faded, but only slightly. "I can guess who it was. That friend of your mother's, isn't it? The romantic one from the jungle. The one with the impossible name. Surely you're not thinking of marrying him, are you? He's hardly your type."

"Who is my type?"

"I am, darling, and you know it. Listen, I'm prepared to be magnanimous about this. After all, you're only human, prey to the same hormonal urges as most people. I certainly won't condemn you for being tempted. After all, you're under a lot of stress.''

''Aren't you prey to hormonal urges?'' she asked, curious.

He shrugged. ''I'm good at sublimating them. There are a great many things more interesting than sex when it comes right down to it. I thought we were agreed on that.''

''You don't want to have sex with me?''

Edward sighed, a long-suffering sound. ''We'll have wonderful, energetic sex, dear one. I've been told I'm very adept. And we'll have children if you want. I have no objections, as long as we can find proper help. And if our marriage ends up as more of a friendship than anything else, then we might count ourselves blessed.''

''And what if I'm tempted again? Fall prey to my hormonal urges?'' She was staring at him in complete fascination. She'd always thought Jake Wyczynski was an exotic creature. He was absolutely normal compared to the man she was supposed to marry.

He smiled sweetly. ''I know I can count on you to be discreet.''

She walked toward him, slowly, and placed her hands on his broad, perfect shoulders. ''No, Edward,'' she said gently. She brushed a sweet kiss against his perfectly shaven cheek. ''I won't marry you.''

For a moment doubt clouded his fine eyes. And

then he shrugged, undeterred. "I'll be waiting for you at the church, Susan. You'll come to your senses. I know you will. What in heaven's name do you think that man has to offer you? A life of roughing it, living out of your suitcase like some gypsy?"

"Goodbye, Edward."

For a moment his perfect features darkened, and she remembered Neddie Marsden's dangerous rage. But that was another time, another man, another life. Chances were it was only a dream.

"You're making a huge mistake, Susan."

"Goodbye, Edward."

And then she was alone, in her mother's house, in her aunt's wedding gown. More alone than she'd ever been in her long, lonely life.

Chapter Seventeen

Susan packed her clothes in a small suitcase. Not her elaborate, designer trousseau, befitting an Abbott. But her jeans and shorts and khakis, her T-shirts and sweaters and hiking shoes. She had no idea where she was going, but it didn't matter. She'd spent her life in Connecticut, in the small, circumscribed world of the Abbotts, afraid to listen to her heart and soul. It was time for her to strike out on her own.

She didn't bother to take off the wedding dress as she moved around her room. It was oddly comfortable—the rich satin flowing over her body, and she hummed beneath her breath, trying not to think of anything but the limitless future.

She was making coffee when the car pulled in the driveway, and she looked up, and froze. It was Jake, alone, in a fast little sports car she'd never seen before.

She had no intention of answering the front door, but it was unlocked, and he slammed it open, looking furious. "What the hell do you think you're doing?" he greeted her.

Considering that the last time she'd looked into his eyes they'd been wrapped around each other, and he'd been deep inside her, the greeting left something to be desired.

"Making coffee," she said.

"Why are you wearing that dress? Why did you leave the garage without a word? Didn't you see my note?"

She shrugged. So he'd left a note, one she hadn't bothered to look for, so certain she'd been abandoned. It didn't matter. It was now or later, and the sooner she got past the pain, the sooner she could get on with her life.

"I'm getting married this afternoon, remember?" It was a lie, but he didn't know that.

He didn't move, but he turned pale beneath his golden tan. "After last night?"

"Today usually comes after the night before, doesn't it?" She concentrated on watching the dark coffee drip through the filter.

"I thought you were going to marry me."

"I didn't think you were serious. You're hardly the marrying kind. Did you mean it?"

There was no reading the expression on his face. He looked at her as if he didn't know her. "What do you think?"

Susan lifted her head and smiled coolly. "I think you're not looking for a wife, or any kind of commitment. So that settles it."

"What about Edward? How will he feel when he finds out…?"

"I already told him. Edward forgives me."

"Big of him," Jake snarled.

"So you're off the hook. You can go back to Timbuktu or wherever you came from and never have to think of me again. I imagine you got any transitory lust out of your system last night. I know I did." It was a lie, of course. Just looking at him made her stomach clench in longing, her knees weak. But she couldn't have him. She knew it. She couldn't change the past, and she couldn't change the future either. At least, not into what she wanted.

He just stared at her. "Pier 18, 37th and 12th," he said. "Eight-thirty."

She jerked her head up in shock, but he was already gone, slamming the door behind him.

She wasted precious moments, frozen, and by the time she moved, racing out the door after him, he was already gone.

She took a cup of coffee, carried it out onto the back terrace and set it down, promptly forgetting about it. How had he known? Fifty years ago Lou Abbott had run to the man she loved, at that very place. Though he had the time wrong—Lou had found Jack at three-thirty.

She closed her eyes, weary beyond belief. Time and truth had faded, and all she wanted to do was run away. Run away with the man she loved.

"What are you doing out here?" Her mother stood in the terrace door, her voice soft and strained. Susan turned to look at her, and a fierce pain went through her heart.

For the first time in her life her mother looked old. Broken, beaten, lost. Susan rose swiftly, pulling her mother's slight figure into her arms. "He's left you again, hasn't he?" she said, furious anger in her voice. "He's abandoned you once more."

"I sent him away."

Susan put her at arm's length, staring down at her. "Why?"

Mary pulled away, running a delicate hand through her soft hair. "I was afraid," she said simply. "I didn't think I could stand losing him again."

Pain and triumph swept through Susan. "If he left once there's a good chance he'll leave again. You made the wise decision, even if it hurts...."

"I made a cowardly decision, just as I did thirty years ago," Mary said bitterly. "I sent him away in the first place. I kept him out of our life, because he drank too much. He's been sober ever since, for more than twenty-five years, and yet I'm afraid to trust him. Afraid to go against my parents' wishes, even though they've been dead for more than twenty years. I wanted him to come back, but there was no way I could ask him. Not after refusing to talk with him for years."

"So why not now? Why send him away now?"

"Because I'm afraid. I'm not like your aunt Lou," she said. "I don't have the nerve to throw everything away for love. And I'm afraid you're just like me."

"But Aunt Lou didn't throw everything away for love, did she?" Susan demanded. "You told me she married Ned Marsden and died. Didn't she?"

Mary didn't answer. "I'm going to lie down for a while. I don't want to think about…"

"When did he leave?"

Mary shook her head. "His flight left this morning. He begged me to let him stay but I told him no."

"You could go after him."

"Don't be ridiculous. I made the wise decision."

"You made the stupid decision," Susan said flatly. "Your sister would be ashamed of you. I'm ashamed of you. Go after him. Catch the next flight to wherever it is he lives, show up on his doorstep wrapped in Saran Wrap and beg his forgiveness. Tell him you made a mistake, and if he still loves you you'll never leave him again."

An odd expression came into Mary's eyes. "What's gotten into you? You've always been so careful, so determined to make the wise decision."

"I'm making the wise decision. I'm not marrying Edward."

"Thank God," Mary breathed.

"And I'm sending you after the man you love. Once you get there it's up to you not to screw it up, but I'm not letting you use me as an excuse. Go after him. Don't waste the rest of your life."

Mary stood stock-still, watching her. And suddenly twenty years fell off her, like a blanket, and she smiled a dazzling smile. She threw her arms around Susan with an exuberance almost foreign to her nature. A moment later she was racing out the front door.

The house grew still and quiet around her. She turned off the telephone, locked the doors and stretched out on the living room sofa, Tallulah's satin gown draped around her. She could only hope Edward had done something about canceling the wedding. Otherwise four hundred guests were converging on St. Anne's Episcopal Church, and there'd be no bride.

Like her mother before her, she'd sent away the right man. And there was nothing she could do about it.

She watched the hands on the grandfather clock move inexorably onward. The clock had come from the old house, as well—she remembered Ridley setting it. It moved past five, then five-thirty, and she breathed a deep sigh of relief. Wondering why she still felt so empty inside.

It was after six when she heard the rumble of the car in the driveway. It sounded like the little sports car that Jake had been driving, and she froze, until she heard the key in the door. She didn't move from her spot on the sofa. Only her mother had a key to the house—she must have chickened out at the last minute. Maybe the two of them could be tiresome old maids together, sharing a house and an empty life.

But it wasn't her mother's footsteps in the hall, moving with slow, stately care toward the living room. A figure appeared in the shadows at the entranceway, tall, stooped with age but still graceful, and Susan stared at her in shock.

"So I travel halfway around the world just for the chance of disrupting another wedding at St. Anne's, and it's all for nothing," the old lady said in a tart, deep voice. "Obviously you have more sense than your mother gave you credit for." She moved into the room, an ebony cane in one gnarled hand, and went straight to the huge leather chair, sinking down with a faint grunt. "I always hated this chair," she said in a conversational voice.

Susan stared at her, unable to move. She was a very old woman, her silvery hair piled high on her aristocratic head, her dark eyes bright with intelligence and the wisdom of age.

"Who are you?" Susan's voice came out in a shocked croak. But she already knew the answer.

The old lady let out a bark of laughter. "That dress looks almost as good on you as it did on me. Though some might call it unlucky. This is the second wedding that didn't go through. Make sure your mother doesn't want to borrow it when she remarries your father, or she might be doomed."

Susan sat up, staring in shock. "Aunt Lou?"

"Of course. Or your godmother Louisa, if you prefer."

"But you're dead. You died in a train crash the day you married Neddie Marsden."

"I never married Neddie. I took off in the middle of the service and went after the man I loved. Of course the family covered it all up with a bunch of lies, and after fifty years not too many people know or care about the truth. Your uncle Jack and I were married on board the *Lizzie B.* and we never spent a night apart for the last forty-eight years until he died.''

''I'm sorry,'' Susan murmured.

''Hell, we wanted to spend those nights together,'' Lou said with a deep laugh. ''Oh, you mean you're sorry he's dead. So am I, love. More than I can say. But he lived a good, full life and he went very fast, so you can't ask for much more. I miss him every day. But Jake looks after me, and I'm old enough to know you can't live forever.''

''Jake?''

''He's Jack's nephew. We brought him up. Never could have children of our own for some reason, so we'd pick up any loose strays we could find. You have about twenty-seven cousins. I may have lost count.''

''Including Jake?'' She felt like Alice after she'd gone through the looking glass, lost in a crazed world where dead women walked and nothing made sense.

''Well, not by blood, of course. That was my past, and there's no way to change the past. You can only change the future.''

''That's what my mother said.''

''Where is she, by the way? I haven't seen her since Jake dropped me off here this morning. I was looking forward to meeting Alex.''

''She sent him away.''

"Silly fool," Lou said with asperity. "I thought she was smarter than that. He's a good man. She shouldn't let him get away a second time. Ridley and Elda were too much for Mary to fight back when you were born. They'd already lost me, and they thought if they convinced Mary to get rid of Alex she would remarry befitting an Abbott. They were wrong, of course. She never stopped loving him."

"She's gone after him."

"Well, thank goodness," Lou said tartly. "Now we just have to figure out how to drum some sense into you. I was sure by the time I showed up here you'd have dumped your fiancé and fallen for Jake. He was my final wedding present for you."

"Fallen for Jake? You mean this has all been some crazy matchmaking scheme? I can't stand the man—he drives me crazy. What makes you think I could ever fall in love with someone like him?"

Lou's smile was full of ancient wisdom. "Instinct. A gypsy in Bulgaria. A shaman in Zaire. A wise woman in Thailand. They all said you two were made for each other."

"New-age crap."

"Old-age crap, my dear. Wisdom from an age far greater than yours. So you're going to tell me you don't care about Jake?"

"Not in the slightest."

"And you usually spend the night before your wedding having sex with people you don't care about?"

"Did he tell you that?"

"He didn't have to. I could tell by that dazed look in his eyes, by the love bite on his throat and by the tone of his voice when he said your name. He's been a son to me, and I know him better than he knows himself. He's in love with you, like nothing he's ever felt before. And it looks like you've decided to break his heart."

"He left me!"

"Pooh! Men leave all the time. If they love you they come back. Do you mean to tell me you threw away love because you're a coward?" Lou rose to her full height, looking very stern. "Haven't you learned anything from the last few days?"

"You know what happened?" Susan gasped.

Lou's ancient, gorgeous face creased in a smile. "You had a dream, Susan. A strange, wonderful dream. And you had it for a reason. Don't ignore the lessons it taught you."

The grandfather clock struck six, a somber tolling, and for a moment Susan was back in the old house, listening to the clock chime her life away. She looked across at the elegant old woman. "Where is he?"

"You know where he is. The ship has a different name, but the berth is the same. You can find him if you hurry."

"I can't—"

"Of course you can. All you have to do is want to."

"My mother took my car. And I need to change my dress—"

"No time, my dear. I brought your cousin's car—

you have just about enough time to jump in and drive into Manhattan before the ship leaves. It still has a manual transmission, but I'm sure you can handle it.''

"What cousin?" she demanded, confused.

"Todd Abbott. He's aged well, the little charmer. I borrowed his Miata—you can drive it into the city and leave it there. He probably won't appreciate losing another car, but I imagine he'll get over it.''

"He didn't die? But I thought you couldn't change the past?"

Lou's smile was enigmatic. "Sometimes we're given blessings." She crossed the room and took one of Susan's hands in her strong, gnarled grip. She pulled her up with surprising force for someone so thin, and for a moment, in the shadowy room, she looked exactly like the reflection Susan had seen in the mirror. Young and strong and beautiful. "Get a move on, girl. It's a family tradition.''

"But what if he doesn't want me?"

Aunt Lou snorted. "He's not that stupid. You need to make a leap of faith, or you'll deserve to live your life with a broken heart.''

She looked at her aging aunt. "Didn't I just do this a couple of days ago?" she asked plaintively.

Lou laughed. "You had a dream, Susan. Time to wake up and live.''

The traffic on the Merritt Parkway was horrendous on a Saturday afternoon, but at least the Miata came equipped with powerful air-conditioning. She drove like a race car driver, fast and dedicated, but it was still close to eight o'clock by the time she crossed the George Washington Bridge.

She'd never been in the docks of Manhattan except in her dream, but they didn't look as if they'd changed much in the past fifty years. There was no place to park, but she didn't care. She simply left the car, keys inside, and grabbed her suitcase in one hand, her satin train in the other, and headed toward Pier 18.

The *Barbara K.* didn't look much newer than the *Lizzie B.* The night was dark around her, and this was hardly the safest section of Manhattan, and if she had any sense at all she'd run back to the car and get the hell out of there.

But she had no sense. The time for smart choices was over. It was time to lead with her heart.

A leap of faith, Aunt Lou had said. And surely Jake Wyczynski was worth it.

The sense of déjà vu was so powerful she almost felt dizzy with it. She found her way to Jake's cabin with no arguments from the busy crewmen, and she found it empty, with a wide bunk, not too dissimilar from the room where Tallulah had spent her honeymoon.

She sat down to wait.

She wondered what she'd do if the boat left before she had a chance to see him. To make sure he really wanted her. But she already knew the answer to that. She'd wait.

He came back to the room just as the *Barbara K.* started out into the harbor. His shirt was unbuttoned and pulled loose from his jeans, his expression was bleak, and he didn't even see her when he first walked in.

"Surprise," she said in a soft voice.

All expression left his face as he stared at her. He kicked the door shut and leaned against it, not moving. "I can't give you what you want," he said finally.

She rose to her knees, the wedding gown pooling around her in the wide bunk. "What do you think I want?"

"Safety. A fancy house in the suburbs, a husband who wears three-piece suits. Two imported cars in the garage, a stock portfolio and an HMO."

"What makes you think I want that?"

"Why else would you marry someone like Edward?"

"I didn't marry him."

"No, I guess you didn't. When did you decide that?"

"Last night."

"But you told me—"

"I know what I told you. You annoyed me."

He had a beautiful mouth, and it curved in a wry smile. "A young woman of my acquaintance told me I can be very annoying. Of course, two hours later she was in bed with me, so maybe I should take that with a grain of salt."

"Maybe some women find annoyance to be an aphrodisiac."

"I don't stay put, you know. I wander from one

place to the next. I'm like Lou and Jack—I don't like settling down for too long.''

''All right.''

''I don't care about money or possessions. Sometimes I'm broke, sometimes I'm rolling in cash. I have a gift for making money, and a gift for spending it. I don't worry about the future, I just take each day as it comes.''

''All right.''

''The only family I have left, the only family I care about, is Aunt Louisa.''

''I thought you had twenty-seven brothers and sisters.''

''She told you that? I do. I call 'em the horde. We all get along well enough, though most of them are more settled than I am. When did you see Lou?''

''She told me to come after you.''

''Are you always so obedient?''

''When I want to be.''

''So what do you want from me?''

It was that simple, and that difficult. She pushed her hair back from her face and took a deep breath.

''I want you to love me,'' she said. ''I want you to love me as much as I love you.''

He didn't even blink. ''Impossible.''

''Impossible?'' she echoed, her heart collapsing.

''There's no way you could possibly love me as much as I love you. I'm out of my mind for you. Demented, obsessed, crazed, and tempted to buy you that damned house in the suburbs and join a firm of stockbrokers. You could never even begin to understand how much I love you.''

''I'm here, aren't I?''

He looked shocked, as if he'd just realized the ramifications of it all. The ship was steaming down the Hudson River, and she was kneeling in his bed, looking up at him with her heart in her eyes.

''Yeah,'' he said, wondering. ''You're here.''

She looked around her. ''Where are we going?''

''Does it matter?''

''No. Not as long as I'm with you.''

He took a breath, and it was almost painful. ''The ship's headed for the coast of Spain then on to Africa. I was planning on leaving there and going across country.''

''Will you take me with you?''

He touched her then. Crossed the cabin and put his hands on her shoulders, pulling her up against his smooth, hot chest. ''Yes,'' he said. ''And I'll never leave you.''

She slid her arms around his neck and kissed him, her heart in her mouth. ''Help me take off this damned wedding dress,'' she whispered, ''and I'll never let you go.''

And he did.

Epilogue

Two years later

The palazzo in Venice had to be her favorite of the seven places they'd lived in their two years of married life together. The farmhouse in Spain ran a close second, and the cottage in the Hebrides had been wonderful, as well.

But the palazzo, tumbledown and damp with mold and rotting plaster, was her absolute favorite. Because her first child was going to be born there.

It was the only place large enough to hold a sizable section of her extended family. Alex and Mary had rooms on the third floor, Aunt Lou had left her villa in Tuscany for a state apartment on the first floor, prepared to await the arrival of the newest member of the family in style. There were at least a dozen half brothers and sisters, all different ages, races, nationalities and sizes scattered throughout the ramshackle building, and Jake divided his time between some obscure project to shore up a section of the sinking city and spending time with his myriad siblings, all of whom uniformly adored him. Not to mention his very pregnant wife.

She never would have thought Jake Wyczynski could be so patient and tender. She never would have thought he'd be exactly what she needed in her life. Someone to annoy and challenge her, someone to nurture her and shove her out on her own. Someone to love her for being Susan, not an Abbott of Connecticut.

It was a perfect autumn day, cool and clear, and even the canals seemed serene. That was what they called the city—La Serenissima. The Most Serene. She could only hope they came back here later on. She'd like all her babies to be born in Venice.

But in the end it didn't matter. Her home was the people she loved, and they were scattered all over the world. As long as she had Jake with her she'd always be at home.

She could hear the thunder of footsteps on the broad staircase, and Jake's shout of laughter as he chased his teenage brothers, Mamoo and Walter, past Aunt Lou's room. From overhead she could hear the ripple of laughter floating down from the balcony outside Mary and Alex's room, and somewhere in the distance a radio was playing opera at a distorting bellow.

She leaned back against the moth-eaten divan and stroked her belly. The pains had been coming, regular as clockwork, for the past two hours, and they were getting close enough together that she knew this time was no false labor. She'd have to go fetch her husband to take her to the hospital, unless Aunt Lou had her way and delivered the baby herself. She insisted she'd delivered more than a hundred children, and Susan believed her, but she still had a nostalgic longing for a real doctor.

For a few minutes more she would simply lie back and listen to the noise all around her, feel the baby move inside her and know that life was very good indeed.

HARLEQUIN®
AMERICAN ◆ ROMANCE®

COMING NEXT MONTH

#769 SUDDENLY A DADDY by Mindy Neff
Delaney's Grooms
Dylan Montgomery was the kind of man who could take anything on the chin. But when Dylan found one of Karl Delaney's infamous notes in his coat pocket that said he would be a daddy, a light breeze could have flattened Dylan. Because the only mommy could be…Karl's niece, Whitney Emerson.

#770 THE HUNK & THE VIRGIN by Muriel Jensen
Being stuck with gorgeous stud Gib London for six weeks was going to be torture for old-fashioned Kathy McQuade. The sexy bodyguard was supposed to be guarding her virtue—not tempting her to abandon it!

#771 THE MOST ELIGIBLE…DADDY by Tina Leonard
Sexy Single Dads
Noreen Cartwright's elderly relatives were on a mission: to get her off the shelf. Since the stubborn young woman wanted no time with a fella, the three ladies set to matchmaking her with Parker Walden—the sexiest man and most eligible daddy Rockwall, Texas, had ever seen!

#772 HOW TO CATCH A COWBOY by Karen Toller Whittenburg
Kurt McCauley had long been a thorn in Emily Dawson's side. But while the too-handsome, too-famous cowboy was pining for Emily's sister, he somehow wound up married to Emily! They'd just have to get an annulment—except, Kurt knew they'd had a wedding night. And might be having a baby…

Look us up on-line at: http://www.romance.net